There was a baby.

She'd been asleep for a whole month.

Riot opened the door just as Krav reached for her, pulling her back against his hard body as it opened to reveal a woman standing there, holding a tiny little bundle, cradled to her chest.

The baby had dark hair, her skin golden. None of Riot was visible at all. She looked for her own features desperately and didn't see any.

She saw *him*.

But there was nothing that decisively stated that she was there as well.

But she felt it. *She felt it*, and she couldn't say what it was.

She knew so little right now. She knew nothing about how she had gotten to this place in her life. And she didn't look at her fiancé and know anything.

But looking at this child, she knew.

Maisey Yates is a *New York Times* bestselling author of over one hundred romance novels. Whether she's writing strong, hardworking cowboys, dissolute princes or multigenerational family stories, she loves getting lost in fictional worlds. An avid knitter with a dangerous yarn addiction and an aversion to housework, Maisey lives with her husband and three kids in rural Oregon. Check out her website, maiseyyates.com.

Books by Maisey Yates

Harlequin Presents

His Forbidden Pregnant Princess
Crowned for My Royal Baby

Once Upon a Seduction...

The Prince's Captive Virgin
The Prince's Stolen Virgin
The Italian's Pregnant Prisoner
The Queen's Baby Scandal
Crowning His Convenient Princess

Pregnant Princesses

Crowned for His Christmas Baby

The Heirs of Liri

His Majesty's Forbidden Temptation
A Bride for the Lost King

Visit the Author Profile page
at Harlequin.com for more titles.

Maisey Yates

THE SECRET THAT SHOCKED CINDERELLA

HARLEQUIN
PRESENTS

HARLEQUIN®
PRESENTS™

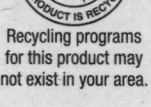

Recycling programs
for this product may
not exist in your area.

ISBN-13: 978-1-335-73862-2

The Secret That Shocked Cinderella

Harlequin Enterprises ULC
22 Adelaide St. West, 41st Floor
Toronto, Ontario M5H 4E3, Canada
www.Harlequin.com

Printed in U.S.A.

THE SECRET THAT SHOCKED CINDERELLA

To the Happiest Place on Earth, which inspired this one while I was on a much-needed family vacation and contributes to my motto: never grow up.

CHAPTER ONE

RIOT PHILLIPS HAD finally done something spontaneous. And it was turning out very, very badly.

Her name, a gift from her hedonistic mother, had never been representative of who she was. She'd been meek and mild all her life. Cleaning up her mother's messes as best she could, and taking all the money in her savings account for a once in a lifetime trip to Cambodia was not in her wheelhouse, at all.

But her roommate Jaia was one of those people you couldn't deny. Infectious and fun and the kind of woman who effortlessly pulled off a nose ring and got new tattoos of a Tuesday, just because. And when Jaia had said she had some old friends from high school headed to Angkor Wat to explore the ruins and go on a spiritual quest, Riot had been caught up in the moment.

She'd looked at her passport, something she had just in case but had never used. She'd looked at her suitcase—also never used. And she'd decided to just say yes.

And everything had been fine. Until they'd hooked up with Jaia's friends. Lilith and Marcianne took everything Jaia was and amplified it. Everything was more reckless, less organized, and significantly drunker and Riot had been on edge for two days. The hostels they'd been staying in might as well have been a street corner—one was a tree house and when their next door neighbors had gotten amorous the whole thing had...swayed.

Worse, Riot hadn't immediately known why.

And it was drunken Lilith who had howled over Riot not immediately guessing that the motion was caused by thrusting.

But the days spent exploring the different towns they'd been in had been incredible, and when Riot couldn't handle the girls, she was happy to go off on her own.

Then they'd gotten to Siem Reap, the town nearest the ruins, last night to find the hostel full, and Marcianne had talked a man at a local bar into offering them his front room, where Riot had spent the whole night petrified.

Then they'd gone to the ruins and Riot had forgotten everything. All the drama, all the chaos. Because it was so beautiful, so serene and somehow every fantasy she'd ever had about...what might be out there. Bigger and bolder and *more* than her small town in Georgia.

It was a ruin, but the rocks had contained more life, more spirit than anything she'd ever encountered and when she breathed, she felt like she was truly breathing for the first time.

And then it had started to rain.

Not just rain...pour down buckets.

The air was thick and steamy, her dress sodden within seconds, she held the hem up, even though it was really too late to keep herself dry—but she was going to try and make a run for it.

And soon she realized...

She had been left.

The tuk-tuk they'd hired was gone, along with Lilith, Jaia and Marcianne.

She ran out of the temple she'd been in, down the front steps, the stone structure looming behind her, no longer peaceful but ominous. The rain seemed to have cleared out everyone and she was...alone.

Well, this felt like a metaphor for about a thousand painful moments in her childhood.

She took out her cell phone and she tried to call Jaia. It went straight to voice mail. Again and again, while she stood there with rain pouring over her skin.

Then she ducked back into the temple, took shelter in the rock there and walked down a long corridor that was partially open to the elements.

She wasn't cold. But she was utterly saturated. She bowed her head low, water rolling forward down her nose. She touched the stone walls, slick now, and wondered if it was really all that different or special being abandoned in Cambodia versus the abandonment she experienced back home.

Sure. You don't know how to help yourself here. That's what's different.

This was what she got for spontaneity. She should have known it wasn't for her. Not ever.

And then she looked up and everything in her froze.

She wasn't alone.

There was a man standing there. Sheets of rain fell between them, keeping her from seeing him clearly, but she could have sworn he was in a white dress shirt and a dark suit, like he was prepared for a meeting.

In temple ruins. In the rain.

He was tall. At least, he felt tall from where she stood.

It was impossible to say from this distance.

He had his hands in his pockets—a confident stance, rather than a casual one, and she wasn't sure why she knew that, only that she did.

She should run.

She was a woman alone, in the rain, whose dress had become near pornographic with the way it stuck to her in this rain. And he was…a man. A Strange Man. Well, not inherently strange, but a stranger.

She didn't run.

She had nowhere to run to.

So, she simply stood.

And then, he was the one who moved.

Graceful and silent, like a tiger stalking its prey. As he moved closer, his features came into view.

His hair was black, his skin golden brown. His face was sculpted with razor sharp cheekbones, a blade straight nose and a mouth that seemed dangerous.

His eyes were dark and mesmerizing, like the rest of him.

Yet again, she thought she ought to run. But didn't.

She'd also been right about him being tall.

Which set off a further alarm bell. If she was right about him being tall, she was probably right about him being a predator.

But she still didn't run.

You can't outrun a tiger...

That was not a helpful thought.

She didn't know what to do. If she should speak, or if she should run. She froze instead. And the tiger began to advance.

"Are you lost?" he asked.

His voice was like the sound a tiger made. All low, and felt in the deepest parts of you. She didn't know whether she wanted to cower in fear or...draw closer to him.

"I'm not lost," she said, her voice absorbed by the moss, plants and soft ground, the damp brick. She sounded small.

"Are you in trouble?"

"My friends left me."

Oh, good. Tell the strange man you're all alone.

"I already know there is no one else here."

"And why are you here?" she asked, feeling bold

in the moment. But only in the moment, because as soon as it passed she asked herself why on earth she was engaging the tiger man in speech.

"I went for a walk," he said. "I live nearby."

"Just…in a suit? Were you at a funeral?" She'd meant it to sound caustic and it had come out more a question.

His head tipped up, as did the corner of his mouth. "Yes."

"Oh. I'm sorry."

He shrugged one broad shoulder and took another step towards her. She'd been hoping that if he did draw closer she would see that she'd exaggerated his size, his masculine energy, his handsomeness.

But no.

He burned brighter, the closer he got.

"Sorry helps nothing," he said.

"It's not about helping. It's just about letting someone know they aren't alone."

But they both were.

Together.

The rain continued to pour and her dress was completely stuck to her body. She became very aware of both her choice to not wear a bra, and the effect the cold was probably having on her body.

As if her thoughts had cued him, he looked her over. The perusal was slow and somehow made her feel…heated.

There was something about him. She felt like she knew him, while at the same time he felt utterly unknown. It was a strange push and pull. Safety mixed with danger in a way she couldn't define.

Not real danger. She felt safer with this man than she'd ever felt before.

The danger was in her.

As if he had awakened something in her she hadn't known was there.

"Well, then since we are not alone, tell me. What sort of friends go off, and leave one of their own stranded in a monsoon?"

She had nothing else to do other than talk to him. He was her only way back to civilization.

Her phone didn't have data, so she couldn't look anything up. She didn't have a backup plan that wasn't…her flaky friends, which she supposed made her an idiot. So why not?

"I don't actually think they're my friends," she said.

And realized that was true the minute she said the words.

"That seems apparent to me."

"Well, Jaia was my roommate. Is my roommate? Back at home. The other two are her friends, and as soon as we got with them…"

"Old friends taking precedence over new. I see."

"I guess so. I mean, I hadn't really realized how much Jaia was…well she's a flake. This whole trip has been deeply disorganized, and once it started raining they left. Or they met men and they left. Or something. With them, who can say?"

"But no one made sure you were all right?"

"More fool me, I was actually seeing to what we'd discussed doing. I was…" It sounded silly now.

"Yes?"

"I saw this as an opportunity to have a spiritual time." It sounded so dumb and immature, it made her feel exposed, especially next to this man who had an air of worldly sophistication about him. She just sounded like what she was. A silly girl. But she wanted him to understand her, as foolish as that seemed. "By myself. I've… My life has been one long series of struggles and I've finally reached a place where I wasn't so… Where it wasn't so hard. I had some money saved up and I thought I'd come here and experience something new. I thought I'd come and feed my soul for a while because I've always been so focused on survival that part of me has been denied."

"I was here for the same reason," he said, looking up, the rain rolling down his face.

He looked back at her, and she was sure he could see straight through her.

"Oh."

It didn't feel silly, then. It felt like, at least she'd been right about one thing.

"I'm Riot," she said. "Riot Phillips."

He smiled then, in earnest. And it did not make him less intimidating. "Krav."

He did not offer a last name.

Krav.

"You live around here?" she asked.

"I live in many places. Wherever it suits me in the moment. I keep a residence here, and that is where I'm currently staying."

He didn't seem like a bohemian wanderer in the way that Jaia did. But then, he'd been at a funeral, so perhaps that was why.

Maybe the suit was the piece of him that was wrong.

And as she looked at him she thought, yes. The suit was wrong. He was not a man who belonged in a suit. He was a man who belonged here. In the ruins. In the jungle. In the rain.

It was funerals that were wrong.

"Are you…were you here for the funeral?"

"Yes. Though I came a few weeks ago when it was clear my mother would not last much longer."

Her stomach twisted.

"Your mother. Oh, I'm so sorry."

She didn't have the kind of relationship with her mother that brought out any warm feelings in her, but she knew, oh, she knew well, that most people loved their mothers very dearly. And in fairness, she loved hers. It was part of why it was so difficult.

If she felt nothing, then it would all be easier. But she did.

"It is life." He looked desolate when he said it, even though his voice didn't change. "A part of it. And never do I feel more aware of that and connected to it than when I am here, so it felt just the right place for a walk."

He was still a tiger.

But she did not think he'd eat her.

In spite of herself, she shivered. It wasn't particularly cold, but the fabric of her dress was truly stuck to her now. And it was beginning to seep down into her bones.

"Come with me," he said. "You're soaked clean through. My home is just a short walk away."

"Your...home is a short walk away?"

"Yes," he said. "Through the trees."

"The trees but..."

"Follow me."

She did, because there was nothing else to do. And because she felt if she didn't...the very thought of not going with him filled her with a sense of sadness. Darkness. And when they came to the end of the ruin, he went on. Deep into the jungle.

The darkness of the foliage swallowed them whole.

"I don't think there's..."

And then she looked up. There was a glow in the trees, and her jaw dropped.

It was a house. Up in the trees. Not at all like the hostel they'd stayed in last week, but something otherworldly. The roots of the trees grew down over the top of a stone shrine, the banyan tree seeming to hold it like a mother would cradle a child, and it was the trees above the shrine that held the house as well, large pillars extending down to the ground, adding support. A staircase began at the shrine and wound tightly around the tree, carrying them up into the canopy, and into the house.

There was an expansive deck around the whole outside of the house, and he led the way to a door that seemed to open by magic. It was ornately carved, as was the rest of the home, and when they were inside, she was stunned by the care given to each exquisite detail. The carvings inside mirrored much of the temple art, and there were grand tapestries hanging on the walls. The living area was plush, with cushions spread all over. There was a small kitchen area off to the side.

"One moment," he said.

He disappeared into another room and returned a moment later with a silk robe on a hanger. "You should get into something that hasn't been rained on, and I can dry your dress."

"Oh, I…"

Her heart thundered wildly and she couldn't quite say why.

"You may change in there." He gestured off to the left, and she found her feet doing his bidding, even while her mind continued to question both him and herself.

She should ask him to call her a car.

She should ask if he could take her back to…to where? They didn't have a hostel booked. But she could find a hostel on her own. With just a little help.

She was going to have to accept that she couldn't count on Jaia and company anyway.

And she would.

After her dress was dry. Because she really was uncomfortable.

When she walked into the room he'd sent her to, it took her a moment to gather her wits because she felt transported. Unlike the front of the tree house, the bathroom was modern, and much more lavishly appointed than she could have imagined a tree house might accommodate.

Who was this man?

She undressed slowly, shivering as she peeled the thin fabric of her dress away from her skin and let it pool at her feet. She realized she was standing naked in a strange man's tree house bathroom and she laughed. She couldn't help herself.

This wasn't the adventure she had imagined going on, but it was an adventure. And maybe that was good enough.

Well, it was happening no matter what, so she supposed what she felt about it was irrelevant.

The robe was luxuriously beautiful. All jade and gold silk with cranes winging their way across the decadent landscape. She had never given much thought to her looks. Being beautiful didn't help her survive and at worst, it attracted the kind of attention from men she just didn't want. But right now, in this strange place in the middle of the jungle, she felt beautiful.

And maybe that should concern her. Because she was alone with a man she didn't know. But she wasn't afraid.

He was still a tiger. It was only she didn't fear what he might do.

She exited the bathroom slowly, holding the edges of the robe needlessly together at her bust line.

And he was there, wearing silk pants in blue, his bare chest on display. She was momentarily stunned by the sight of him. Lean, hard cut muscle exposed and gleaming in the light. Every ridge, every dip, was cut hard and well defined.

And there he was, lounging on the cushions, a pot of tea and two cups in front of him. As if he weren't lethal.

As if he weren't the most beautiful thing she had ever seen.

Krav, he said his name was Krav. His accent wasn't Cambodian, but something else. She'd never heard the name before. But then, few people had heard hers. She could see the legacy of this beautiful country in some of the angles of his face. He seemed like a man who might fit anywhere and nowhere all at once. Like he could find a way to be a part of any culture. But at the same time…he would always be separate.

He was too singular to blend.

"Come," he said. "Have a warm drink."

Outside she could still hear the rain pounding down, hard and insistent.

"All right."

She crossed to where he sat and lowered herself down onto the pillows across from him.

"So you came here for a spiritual quest? Did you imagine it might earn you clout on the internet to take selfies at a sacred ruin?"

She shook her head. "No. I'm not on the internet. Not like that. I've never traveled before and it seemed like an amazing opportunity."

She was about to say something caustic about how it had turned out. But the truth was…it was turning out well. This moment was one she would never forget. As she sat there with this man's eyes trained on her, giving her closer attention than she could remember ever having before, she felt…like this was the adventure she'd come for, without realizing it.

Krav was the adventure.

He poured her a cup of tea and handed it to her. His fingertips brushed against hers.

She suddenly felt warm and didn't think it was to do with the tea.

"You are a strange little thing," he said, just as she raised the cup to her lips.

"Am I?" She asked, lowering the cup quickly. "I thought I was simply unremarkable."

"How can a woman called Riot ever think of herself as unremarkable?"

Maybe it was the man, maybe it was the moment. But she wanted to tell him. Everything.

"The name only adds to it. People expect someone wild and I'm not that at all. My mother was the child. There wasn't room for two of us."

"I see."

"The name is hers. Not mine. It's about her."

"You could change it," he said.

"Yes. Though there is something…defiant maybe, about keeping it. And continuing to be me."

The corner of his mouth turned upward. "Ah, yes. Now that I am familiar with."

She sipped her tea, and it was the waves of understanding that seemed to grow between them that surprised her most of all. She shouldn't have anything in common with him. But she felt like he might understand her better than any other person she'd ever met.

The hours went by quickly. They didn't talk about deep things. And yet the things they did speak of— favorite foods from their childhood, the seasons they liked best, all uncovered pieces of who they were. And it felt deep. It felt real.

And when he leaned across the space between them and kissed her, it wasn't like kissing a stranger. Because he wasn't a stranger. She knew him better than she'd ever known another person.

Krav who lived in the trees.

Krav whose mother was gone.

Krav, who kissed like a dream but was real. So very real. Warm and far too sharp and hard to bear. He burned bright, and so did she. Like the tiger had taken her for his own, not to eat, but to claim.

She'd never been kissed before. It came back to

the fact that she had never trusted men and never wanted to.

Her mother had made a mess of her life over men and Riot had wanted…independence. Freedom. But she'd never felt half so free as she did right now, kissing this stranger in the trees.

His movements were expert, his hand on her cheek warm, his thumb sliding over her cheekbone and creating a hot sensation that started there but rioted through her. Down to her chest, down between her thighs. Until she burned, all of her.

"Krav," she whispered.

His dark eyes burned into hers and she trembled. And she understood now why people made crazy decisions in the name of desire. Why Jaia was always tragic about some man or another. Because this moment, where she'd met a stranger in the rain and gone back to his house, seemed perfectly reasonable and somehow in the back of her mind she knew that it shouldn't.

But it didn't just seem reasonable, it seemed necessary. To part her lips for him and allow greater access. To let him slide his tongue against hers and taste her like she was an indulgent dessert.

She felt like an indulgent dessert. Or maybe a whole riot, contained in a girl who had never felt anything like that at all.

He tugged the shoulder of her robe down and the slick fabric fell away, revealing her shoulder and then, her breast. She might have gasped in shock if it didn't seem natural. If it didn't seem like exactly what was supposed to happen next.

Her nipple beaded tight and his eyes sparked with interest. And she felt…

She had never wanted a man's attention before, not particularly. And so being the unexpected focus of his was something she could scarcely comprehend, much less anticipate.

And it was everything. He was everything.

This was the moment.

That certainty whispered inside of her. A core truth of everything she was.

This was why she had come.

Maybe it was why she had been born.

To feel beautiful under the hands of this man. To feel the exquisite pleasure that came from his hot lips trailing over her neck, down to her shoulder, her breast. The way the tip of his tongue traced the edge of her tightened nipple, before sucking it deep into his mouth.

Her head fell back and she moaned with pleasure. She hadn't really understood pleasure until now. Arousal, sure. But this was different. He was in control. He was the one giving it. Determining the pace and pressure. Where he touched less, where he tasted. How deep. How glorious.

This was her giving the power over to him, and somehow feeling all the more powerful in return.

Riot wrapped her arms around his neck and kissed his cheek. He pulled his head back and looked at her, intensity shining in his gaze. And then he kissed her mouth again. Hard, intense. And she fell back into the cushions, guided by his strong arms, making her feel weightless. Like she was floating.

His kiss was devouring and she had to laugh because perhaps he was going to eat her after all...

And that slightly amusing thought turned molten when he began to kiss a trail down her body, separating the sides of the robe as he went until he was between her thighs, his hungry gaze trained on the most intimate part of her. And then he put his mouth there.

She arched against him, a scream rising in her throat. This was beyond her fantasies. This was beyond anything. The tiger had indeed come to devour her. And she had been right not to run away.

His tongue and fingers created magic in her. Left her breathless. Left her writhing beneath him and begging. He turned her inside out. Made her question things she had never questioned before, all over the stroke of his tongue against her sensitized flesh.

He moved his large hands beneath her rear and held her up, a pagan offering for his consumption. And yet the pleasure was all hers.

The climax overtook her like a wave, and when it shattered her she was left spent and breathless, trying to cling to something, anything that would keep her grounded to the earth.

Krav was all there was.

Then he was above her, his dark eyes intense and

she realized he was naked now, his beautiful body on display in the dim light of the room, the dips and hollows of muscle and glistening golden skin sending her to a place past thought.

But she didn't get a chance to look at him for as long as she wanted before he was over her, settling between her thighs. And then he thrust into her and caught her gasp of pain on his lips. It was a shock.

But he didn't seem to notice, and it didn't take long for the feeling of impossible fullness to begin to recede, giving way to the same pleasure she'd found beneath his mouth but...different.

They were connected. And hadn't she felt like she knew him better than she had ever known anyone only moments before?

That had been nothing compared to this.

They were like one. And the beauty of it, the immense physicality of it, made her want to cry. And she couldn't imagine this thing being traded cheaply around clubs and after dinner dates, she simply couldn't. Because that wasn't what this was. It wasn't cheap or easy or tawdry. Not to her. And it never could be.

It was beautiful, magic. Meant to be.

And in her whole life she had never felt meant to be. She felt like a mistake, and always had. At every moment, at every turn. Like an unwanted tagalong to someone else's experiences. But not this. He needed her for this.

He needed her now.

And as he began to tremble right along with her, as his desire began to match with hers in a desperate race to the finish, she knew then she had never felt so whole. So complete.

Like she belonged.

In the world.

In the moment.

And then her pleasure became a living thing, taking flight inside of her and sending her to the stars before bringing her back down to earth, a sanctuary of glitter and his strong arms holding her steady and keeping her from shattering completely.

She clung to him, and his own movements became fractured, uneven, and when he found his release, it sent her to heights her own had not.

In that moment, he needed her.

He needed her.

And she had never felt so alive. So herself.

He needed her so many times that night she lost track. There on the cushions in the living room, and then in his room, with a large canopied bed.

And she would never again misunderstand what that motion next door might be. Though she would say now, it was weak in comparison to what she'd experienced.

Krav was a dream. A fantasy.

One she didn't want to wake up from.

But when morning came, he was there, looking at her like she was a revelation. And so she stayed. And stayed.

The days and nights melted together, and she began to think that this might be everything.

By the time she was able to get a hold of Jaia, she told her that she wouldn't be finishing the trip with her.

Because she had met a man.

And it was so satisfying to be the one to have found someone. To be the one having a wild, delicious affair.

To be the one falling in love.

Krav was beautiful. Her Tiger. This man who had taken everything she thought she knew about herself and upended it. They stayed in the tree house for a while. But then after that, he took her to a brilliant hotel in Siem Reap, and they got reservations at the most coveted table in the entire country, where she was served gourmet delicacies that thrilled and delighted her.

"We should go to Europe," he said.

She had left her waitressing job before the trip, it was always easy enough to get hired for another job like that, at least it had been for her.

There was the apartment, but that was taken care of until she and Jaia were meant to come back from Cambodia.

There was no reason to not pack up and go with him. Anywhere. Everywhere.

"I feel like there's so much about you I don't know," she said. "And I have told you everything about my life."

"Surely not everything," he said, grinning as he held a bite of chocolate cake up as a temptation across the table. "I am absolutely certain there is more that I don't know."

"There is certainly no more to be seen."

She was shameless with him. And she had never imagined that she could be shameless. But he lit her on fire, from the inside out. Turned her into a stranger, and she wanted to stay this stranger.

This woman who was wild and sensual, who had no boundaries in bed with this glorious, gorgeous man who ignited need within her with a simple look across the room.

But she knew that she was living in a fantasy. Around the edges of this, that reality hovered.

He had to have a job. He had to have a real life. And she was beginning to sense that it wasn't here. But he was not forthcoming with information about himself at all.

"I do have work," he said after they'd spent a week in that glorious hotel. "But I tend to do it while you sleep. And yes, soon… Soon I will need to get back to life. But for now…"

"But what is that life?"

"It is none of your concern."

And that should've been the first indicator to her that it was not for him what it was to her.

But as one week turned to another, and another, from England to France to Switzerland, she forgot to be cautious. She forgot about Jaia. She forgot about her apartment.

About the life she'd walked out of like it was nothing.

She was in love. Quite simply for the first time in her life, she was desperately in love.

One day he looked at her across the bed they shared.

"We should go to Italy for a while."

It occurred to her then, he was Italian. And while she realized that he must be Cambodian in part, and he spoke Khmer with ease, the accent of his English had been different than the ones she'd heard in Siem Reap.

He was Italian.

They went and stayed at an estate on the Amalfi Coast, and it was the most blindingly beautiful place she had ever seen.

And every day, she fell more desperately in love with him.

But it wasn't until she missed her period that she began to be concerned.

Because she wouldn't be unhappy if she was pregnant with his baby. But she was afraid… She was very afraid that he would be.

He was wonderful to her. Always. Even though he worked more now that they were in Europe, it was always gourmet meals and sex all night with Krav.

He was insatiable. Completely and utterly and she loved it.

But she was no closer to knowing him than she had been before, no matter how much she liked to tell herself otherwise. No matter how much she liked to tell herself that she must know him because she knew every inch of his body. Because she knew how to bring him to pleasure. How to make him lose control. Yet no matter how much she tried to tell herself all of that, she didn't think he was going to receive news about a baby easily.

It was that darkness she sensed beneath it all. That predator.

There came a point when she couldn't ignore the missed period any longer, so while Krav was working she went into the village and procured herself a pregnancy test from a drugstore. She went into the bathroom and took the test. And when it came back positive, she began to cry.

She was happy. She was. But she had a terrible feeling that it wouldn't be easy.

She dressed herself up as perfectly as she could. He had provided her with the most beautiful clothes. And she had his chef prepare a dinner that she knew was his favorite.

It was such a funny thing, that she felt she could ask the chef to prepare something specific. She wouldn't have done that even a week and a half ago, but she was beginning to become so settled into the life that they'd made. Is it a life if you still know nothing about him?

She just had to hope that tonight he revealed that he had the same attachment to her that she did to him.

There was a storm starting to rage, and she thought it was ominous. Though it must be either a good omen or a very bad one. Good possibly because this was how they had met. Bad because... Well, typically, a storm didn't signal anything good.

But the table was set beautifully, his favorite pasta dish prepared to perfection.

And she had tried to make herself as beautiful as possible. As if there was a threshold that might make this all okay.

When he walked in, for a moment he looked so dark it stole her breath away. But then he looked at her and smiled.

"Dinner and you. What have I done to deserve this?"

"I just wanted to have a special evening."

"Then a special evening we shall have."

Outside, it was pouring rain now.

They sat down to dinner, and she waited, with all of her nervous energy, trying to force herself to eat so that he wouldn't think something was wrong.

"I have something to tell you," she said.

He looked up at her over the table, and she knew. Before she even spoke, she knew.

That he'd always had the power to devour her if he wanted.

To destroy her.

And that he would.

"I'm pregnant."

His fury was immediate. Like a lit match. And when he moved, he was that Tiger. Instantaneous. Powerful. He was across and standing in front of her in no time at all.

"You're what?"

"I'm pregnant."

"No. That cannot be."

"It's true. You didn't use a condom the first night we were together. How can you say that isn't true? I think there've been many times since then when you haven't."

And the girl she had been back when they had first met would've been embarrassed to talk about this, but not the woman she had become. "How can you look at me and say that there isn't a way?"

"Because it isn't acceptable. I do not want a child."

"Well, I am having one. So now it is simply a question of…"

"No. I want nothing to do with it."

"You can't mean that."

"I do. You don't know anything about me, and that is by design. I will never, never have a child."

And before she could think about what she was doing, she stood and pushed away from the table.

"Riot…"

"Don't talk to me," she said. "Don't touch me. How dare you. *How dare you.*"

"For all I know you're pregnant with someone else's bastard and you're trying to fob it off as mine."

"How dare you," she whispered.

And then she turned and ran out of the room. Ran out of the house. The rain was pounding, but she ran anyway. But she slipped and fell onto the cobbled stones. And felt a violent cramp in her stomach.

She stood up, a sob on her lips. And she felt warmth on her legs.

"Riot," he shouted.

"Go away," she said, tears pouring down her face. "I'm losing it anyway. Everything is lost."

He picked her up and carried her inside. He put her in the shower, then wrapped her in a towel and tucked her into bed.

He left her there.

The next morning he was gone.

But a car arrived for her.

Ready to whisk her into the heart of the village.

And he wasn't there to say goodbye to her. He was gone, her bright burning tiger.

This was over.

When she arrived at the hotel—one of his—there were instructions waiting. She could stay there as long as she wished, and then after the concierge would arrange for her to go anywhere she wanted.

She thought of her tiny apartment back in Georgia.

She had shared it with Jaia but she'd abandoned it—and her—for this life in Europe, like it wouldn't have an end. But it had.

She had no job to go back to.

But now she could go anywhere. Do anything. And Krav had given her the key to that, even as he'd crushed something in her she thought she'd never get back. It felt like a metaphor and one she was going to seize.

She had the ticket. She just needed to be brave enough to take the first step.

She'd been lost in a fairy tale for a moment, lost in pleasure. It was over now, but there was something beyond that.

But if she'd learned one thing in life it was that she couldn't waste her time, her energy or her emotions on other people. He didn't want to be in her life.

Better than that, he'd given her the path to a new one.

This was the journey she'd been brought here to go on. She just hadn't known it.

And so she went to England, because she'd always wanted to go. She'd started in London and ended up going north, to a small village where she worked in a café and got to know everyone.

She went to a doctor, where she found out she hadn't miscarried after all.

She'd bent at the waist, sitting on the medical table and wept. Joy. Sorrow. All cascading through her like endless rain.

How was it possible?

A baby. The baby wasn't gone. Krav was gone. The life she'd thought they would have, that was gone.

Because the man she'd thought he was…he didn't exist.

But this child did.

Her child.

Hers.

Not Krav's.

Just hers.

The doctor held her hand while she cried, and then he gave her a bunch of pamphlets explaining her every option. She took them all, because it seemed responsible. But she didn't need to look at options.

She was keeping the baby.

And she wasn't even afraid. She'd found a life, a community. The older woman she rented a room from had been sweet and nonjudgmental, happy for her in a way Riot knew her mother certainly wouldn't have been.

It would be okay. Everything would be okay. She'd do just fine here in this little village that had adopted her as their American mascot. They liked her accent and they liked her. And this was all part of the new adventure she was on. One that was certainly happier and more filled with hope than anything before it had been.

Everything was perfect—except sometimes she thought of Krav and the heat between them.

And how he'd broken her heart in ways she didn't think she'd ever recover from.

She'd trusted him. In a way she'd never trusted another person. Enough to be naked with him. Enough to feel safe. She'd finally believed…

She'd finally believed love was possible. That for her, it was possible.

The realization that it wasn't had nearly destroyed her. But now she had a new reason to put herself back together. And so she did.

Everything was perfect—except one morning she went to pick up fresh baked scones from a bakery down the street to bring to the café and she was hit head-on by a reckless driver.

Everything was perfect—until she lost consciousness and a swirling darkness claimed her as its own.

CHAPTER TWO

"Mr. Valenti, it's about the girl."

Kravann Valenti looked across his desk at the man standing there. And then looked behind him, at the expansive view of Rome in all its bustling glory. He was tired of Rome.

He was tired of everything.

He had been tired of everything until he'd met Riot Phillips.

She had been standing in the ruins like fate that night, and he had been the fool who'd decided to grab hold of her.

Unexpected. And he had been in a low place in his life, and he was utterly furious he had allowed anyone into that moment.

He had no one to blame but himself.

Perhaps his father had been right after all. Perhaps there was weakness in him after all. A weakness that had needed to be beaten out of him.

It didn't work, did it?

She had wrecked his life.

She had been all he'd wanted, all he'd craved. He'd never been like that, not with anything. Control mattered above all else, and he had none with her.

He'd never kept a woman beyond a weekend, and Riot had been with him a month. One month of sex. He hadn't been able to get enough of her.

Then she had told him she was pregnant.

If there was one thing he had always known it was that he would never have children. And suddenly she didn't seem like simple fate. She seemed like a twist of it. The enemy of everything he'd built. Of all that he'd sworn to be or not to be.

He was not a man who did regret. And yet regret had been his very breath since that night. She had run from him, like he was a monster. And then she had fallen.

Everything is lost.

He'd known then he had to let her go. Because he had never thought he was his father, and that moment had brought him closer than he'd thought possible.

The darkness in him…it had won out.

The image of her there, bleeding, weeping…

It woke him at night.

Shook him awake with its insistence. Evidence of his demons. Demons he would never escape no matter how much he wished he might.

He had not personally looked into what Riot was doing since she had gone. But he had asked that his people keep watch on her.

The Valenti Company was the only reason his father had ever had anything to do with him. A man at his wit's end after his oldest and only legitimate son had died, he'd gone to Cambodia and stolen his bastard from the arms of Krav's mother, making him the heir to the family fortune.

It was not because Sergio Valenti had any soft feelings for a son. It was because he believed in carrying on the family business, and believed it had to be done by Valenti blood.

And he had been the only other direct line to his father remaining.

It had given him much.

Money, education, power.

But it had taken a vast amount from him as well.

His mother had loved him.

But she had been powerless to stand against the powerful Valenti Company when it came to defending her rights to her child.

Krav himself had been five.

He could scarcely remember anything before coming to Italy.

Just vague pictures of a room with bright pink walls and a soft voice speaking to him in his native language.

Then he'd been thrust into a world with unfamiliar nannies, words he didn't understand and a distant, tyrannical father.

He'd survived it. And he'd thought he'd survived it well.

His mother remained his one weakness. He ached

for her, all of his life. Like there was a hole in his chest where his heart had once been. It caused him pain, always. His father had been quick to point out that pain like that was nothing more than human frailty, and Valenti men could not surrender to such things.

He had only done so with her.

Her death had…

It had rocked him in a way he had not imagined anything could. And then Riot had been there.

Riot. A ridiculous name for a girl with blond hair and an accent thick and sweet like honey. She had looked like a forest nymph with her hair all curled from the rain and her brightly colored dress plastered to her body by the rain, her cheeks pink from the sun, her nose scattered with freckles.

And her touch had been a revelation.

He had felt more in those moments with her than he could recall feeling in the whole of his life.

He gritted his teeth and kept his focus determinedly on the scene below. "What about her?"

"She has been injured."

"What?" he turned sharply, and for the first time really looked at the man delivering the message.

But it was not his face he saw.

It was Riot.

Her face full of joy and wonder as she'd looked at the tree house. At him. At everything.

And then devastated that night…that last night.

Injured.

He thought of her lying on the ground, broken. Then he thought of that night he'd broken her. That night all his poison had spilled out and destroyed the world they'd lived in.

Dio, what had he been thinking?

Those months with her. All sun and sex and brightness and he'd been pretending. It had only been a matter of time before the darkness leaked out of him, and it had.

From the first time he'd seen her to the last, she'd gone from pure joy to pure anguish. And it was him. All him.

She was hurt now, though.

And all he could think of was going to her.

"When?" he asked.

"This morning. She was in an accident. She has been living in a village in the north of England."

He asked the question he feared the answer to most. "Is she going to live?"

"It is not certain." He felt that like a blow. "She's unconscious."

He was moving already. "Get the helicopter ready. We are going to England." He had to see her. He had to go to her.

He would not touch her, not again.

But he had to go to her.

"Yes, *signore*. But…there is one more thing."

"What?"

"She's pregnant."

The words rang in his ears like a gong. "Pregnant?"

"Yes."

She hadn't lost the baby.

It had been eight months since he'd seen her. She could have met any number of men in the time since then. Gotten pregnant in the time since she had lost the child she had carried with him.

But he could not ignore the feeling that raced through his veins when he heard the word. Something primal. Something like the beat of a drum that surpassed thought and reached down to the very heart of him.

To a place that defied reason and logic.

His.

That child was his.

All was not lost.

He had not broken this.

And this was his second chance. One he did not deserve, and perhaps…

Perhaps one he should not claim.

He had been more monster than man that night.

But she was unconscious in a hospital, and she was carrying his child.

And monster or man, it mattered not.

She was his.

The man spoke in hushed, apologetic tones. "They do not know if the child will live, either."

If he hadn't sent her away she would not be hurt.

If he hadn't sent her away, the child would be alive.

They had to live.

Both of them.

He would fix this. He was not simply a man, monster he might be. But he was a Valenti. And a Valenti did what must be done.

He would move heaven and earth.

He would take the pen straight from the hand of God and he would damn well write a new ending.

"We are going to England now."

When Riot woke up, she wasn't in her bed.

That was her first thought as she groggily opened her eyes and tried to find a comfortable position. She couldn't. Her arm wasn't mobile and there was a strange beeping sound. And she…ached.

Her eyes fluttered open and she realized she was in what might have been a hospital suite. Except it was…fancy. But there was no denying there was medical equipment everywhere.

She tried to remember how she'd gotten there, but she couldn't. She tried to remember…

She had to call Jaia.

Her roommate would come and get her. Heaven knew she couldn't rely on her mother.

She and Jaia were supposed to go to Cambodia in a couple of weeks. Jaia had decided to go and meet some of her friends on a whim and she'd invited Riot to come along and Riot had thought…why not.

She felt a stab of disappointment. Depending on how badly hurt she was she might not be able to go on the trip.

Maybe it hadn't been such a great idea anyway. After all, it would have cost her so much of her savings.

But then…

She had never really done anything adventurous before. Her life was just…

She had tried so hard not to be her mother. Not to be a riot, really. And somewhere in there she'd become a gray, pale nothing.

One that was in a hospital bed, though.

She looked around, trying to see if she could find a button to push to call a nurse or…someone. As she did she took in more details of the room.

It looked like a bedroom. Though, not an ordinary one. It was luxurious. With deep red wallpaper textured like velvet and gold edging on all the doorposts.

If she weren't in a hospital bed, if there weren't beeping machines and IVs and all of the other medical accoutrements, she wouldn't have ever thought she was in a hospital.

Where was she?

For a moment she knew a zip of fear because this wasn't…normal. And no matter how hard she tried she couldn't remember how she'd gotten here. She couldn't remember the last thing she'd done.

Well, she had a most recent memory. She was in her apartment eating cereal for dinner and listening to Jaia talk about how staying in hostels was fine and she'd done it all through Europe and they'd be perfectly safe.

But that didn't connect to this moment.

It didn't explain how she'd gotten here.

She finally found the call button, or what she thought might be one, and pressed it. Repeatedly. Desperately.

The door opened and in swept a woman, not in a hospital uniform, but in a…pinafore that reminded her of something she'd seen in period pieces, down to the starched white apron.

"Ms. Phillips, you're awake!"

"Yes," she said, feeling groggy and confused. "I you know my name?"

That wasn't actually weird, of course she did. It was probably on all her patient information. She'd surely had her ID with her at the time of whatever accident she was in. But she didn't seem…injured. She was sore, but she wasn't bandaged or anything.

She touched her face just to be sure.

Not a bandage on there, and no blood or anything on the extremities she could see.

"Of course." She raced over and began to look at the machine, and as she did she took her phone out of her pocket—a piece of tech that seemed incongruous with her old-fashioned outfit—and dialed a number quickly. "Yes, Doctor, she's awake. Please come as quickly as you can."

A hard knot of fear began to grow at the center of her chest.

"Is my being awake…a bad thing?" she asked.

"Not at all." The nurse—Riot now assumed she was a nurse—looked down at her. "But it is a bit of a surprise."

"Why?" Fear was now a desperate, living creature clawing at her chest. "Why is it a surprise?"

"Ms. Phillips… I should wait until the doctor gets here to speak more of it."

The door opened again and Riot thought it must be the doctor.

But it wasn't.

It was a man. Tall and broad, dressed in a black suit. His hair was jet black as a raven's wing, his eyes nearly as dark. His skin bronzed, his cheekbones razor sharp, his nose a finely honed blade. He was striking in a way that stole her breath.

He was utterly singular and unique and yet…

And yet something echoed in her soul. A recognition.

But she had no idea who this man was. None at all. She'd never seen him before in her life.

But when he stepped into the room she felt it. Like a seismic wave moving through her body. He brought with him a new pull to the earth, a shift in the stars.

He was power.

She knew it, intuitively. She didn't have to know who he was to know that.

He was more than a man. He was…

A tiger.

That thought came from nowhere and whispered

in her mind, in her soul. Goose bumps spread over her arms and she rubbed at them.

"Mr. Valenti, I don't think—"

But one look from him and the nurse's words fell into silence.

Then he looked back at her and if she hadn't already been stuck in bed, his stare would have pinned her there.

"You are awake," he said, his voice deep, with a beautiful accent that begged the listener to draw closer to him.

Even as everything in her screamed danger.

"Y-yes," she said. "I am awake. As this woman here has observed. And called for help. But I'm not sure why it's significant? Or why…or what happened. Or…or anything."

One of his dark brows winged upward. "You don't know what happened?"

"I don't. And I have no idea why I'm here or who you are."

He seemed to not know what to say to that and she knew—somehow, like she knew anything about him—that he was not a man accustomed to not knowing.

"Riot," he said, her name rough on his lips, sending a shattering sensation through her.

He knew her name, her first name, and why that seemed to make such a difference, she had no idea.

"Riot," he repeated. "You've been unconscious for a month."

"A…a month? That's impossible. I was planning to go on vacation with my roommate and then I woke up here."

"You've already been on vacation with your roommate," he said.

She frowned. "No…no I haven't. I've never been outside the country before."

"And which country do you think you're in now?" he asked.

"I'm in America," she said. "Georgia, I would assume. Where I've lived all my life."

"No, Riot. You're in Rome. In my estate. And you are to be my wife."

CHAPTER THREE

SHE WAS AWAKE, and she did not know him.

The fact was, Krav now had the perfect opportunity to send her away. She didn't remember him. She didn't remember Soriya.

But he had told her she was to marry him anyway.

Kravann Valenti did not second-guess himself. He had not been raised that way. At least not in the second part of his life. His father had been a mean, dictatorial bastard. To make him strong, he'd said.

To make him worthy of the name Valenti.

And Krav had never once acted with the intent to honor his father. It was simply he could never allow his father to be right.

He could not allow his father's fears of Krav's weakness to have any bearing on reality. The only time he had ever shown softness was in the hours following his mother's funeral. When he'd found this creature who lay before him now.

There was a reason he'd sent her off, and quickly.

But now she was here.

And he had just told her she was staying.

But it was no matter.

He had done well enough with the child so far. He had nannies… But why continue on having nannies when the child could have her mother. He had been incensed when he had found the adoption brochure in her things. She had been going to give his child up, without ever giving him a chance to be a father. Not that he knew anything about being a father, but it was the principle of the thing. A child should have their parents. And one of those parents should not be a maniacal sociopath hell-bent on nothing more than the upkeep of his name.

One thing he knew for certain, he wanted Soriya to have her mother. He needed Riot to protect Soriya from his darkness. To act as a buffer.

And she didn't remember anything…

And what of when she does?

It wouldn't matter. By the time she did remember—if she ever did, things would be different.

He was rewriting the story.

After all, she did not have his full name. So it was likely she had only been considering giving the child up for adoption because of financial reasons. As his wife, she would have everything she could have ever wanted and then some.

"I'm… I'm to be your wife?"

"Yes," he said. "You do not remember me, *cara mia*?"

She shook her head, and he was astonished to see her eyes filled with tears.

"What is it?"

"I can't believe I don't remember falling in love. I cannot believe that I don't remember that somebody in this world loves me."

And if he were another man, he supposed he might feel guilt in this moment. Because there was no love between them. Certainly, passion had flared that night in the tree house. There was no denying that.

But love?

Krav did not even know what that was.

He felt a fierce protectiveness for Soriya that he had never felt for any other creature on this earth. A kind of protectiveness that transcended his own sense of self-preservation. It was like having a part of him walking out in the world. He would not characterize that as love. For it was not pleasant.

It made him even more feral, if such a thing were possible.

And when it came to keeping his child's mother here... Well, he would do anything to accomplish that. No guilt involved at all.

"Please," the nurse said. "Mr. Valenti, with all due respect, we must have a doctor here to examine her. She needs an MRI. We need to ensure that she is not placed under any distress."

"This is not a soap opera," he said. "I can hardly see what knowing a little bit about her life is going to do as far as damage goes."

This nurse... She knew nothing about their circumstances. Everybody working in the house at the moment was under the strictest confidence. He could not have the broader world knowing about Soriya, not yet. She was a month old now and had never been taken away from the estate grounds.

And, in spite of the fact that he himself understood few emotional connections, he had made sure that she had been brought into Riot's room every single day by one of the nannies. If there was one thing he knew… It was that a child needed his mother.

He had done. Badly.

And so he had made sure that Soriya had known her mama. And that she had understood she was merely sleeping. Taking a very long nap.

And now she was awake.

"Valenti…" She closed her eyes, and she looked dizzy.

"Do not tax yourself," he said.

On one score he did agree with the nurse, he could not immediately tell her about the baby. She did not remember anything after her trip to Cambodia, then he imagined the child would be quite the shock.

The DNA test had already confirmed that the child was his, so there was no question as to the fact that she had conceived her during that night.

And as she had no memory of that night…

It would be likely she would find the whole thing impossible.

If she found it distressing that she had missed falling in love… If only she knew. That there was no love between them, only a broken, dark passion that had exploded that night. And had undone everything he had ever believed about himself.

He was a man of great control, but never once had he thought of using protection with her.

He had her over and over again that first night, and he had not thought of it.

The doctor arrived shortly after, and examined her. "In theory," he said, "she is in good health."

He was speaking Italian, and Krav had the realization that Riot wouldn't be able to understand. But that would give him the chance to explain after, and be yet further in control of the narrative, and that suited him just fine.

"So there is no reason to withhold information from her?"

"No," the doctor said slowly. "At least, not in my opinion."

"Good."

"I want to check in with her from time to time, and you must keep me apprised as to her memory."

"Yes," Krav said, waving a hand. "But now I feel that we should be left."

"I assume you do have things that must be handled between the two of you."

"Yes. A great many things."

During the visit with the doctor, Riot had gotten out of bed. They had exercised her while she was in a coma, which had ensured that her muscles were not entirely atrophied. And while she had been unsteady on her feet, and required the use of a walker, it had not taken long for her to begin to move around on her own. "I remember how to walk," she had said. "I remember everything except… I guess I don't remember the last…"

"Ten months at least," he said. "Your trip to Cambodia happened that long ago. And you've been in a coma for a month."

"We met there?" She asked, perched up in bed, only the two of them in the room.

And he was surprised then, how much he still wanted her.

He had managed to shut down the ache while she was unconscious. And while he still felt… Something, every time he was near her, he had managed to transfer those feelings to his desire for Soriya to know her mother.

Now he was there, he could not deny that his desire for her was as it had always been. Purely, deeply sexual.

And now was not the time to ponder it.

"I went to Cambodia," she said, softly, not looking at him.

"Yes, you did."

"I can't believe I had a whole adventure and I don't even remember it."

"Well, *cara*, you are still on an adventure."

Her head whipped around and her eyes widened. "That's right. I'm in Rome, aren't I? And I assume you don't mean Rome, Georgia."

"I do not," he said, looking at her.

He had grown accustomed to her face, but sleeping. She had looked peaceful these months, lying in bed as if she were under an enchantment. The doctors had held little hope of her waking, but he had been unwilling to give up on her.

Soriya needed her mother.

And what do you need?

Need.

It burst through him like a bomb.

His need for her.

She was here. Speaking to him. Not just asleep. He felt like part of himself had woken up too.

She wasn't looking at him like he had just broken her whole world.

She was looking at him like she had that first day.

That was what he had, here and now. A second chance at a first day with her.

"I'm actually in Italy. With a man and I'm…engaged." She looked at him as if she was trying to place him. "How did we meet?"

"We met at the temple ruins," he said, deciding to keep the conversation as honest as possible.

But it was clear Riot wanted love. He didn't have the ability to give it to her. But it cost him nothing to weave a new story for them. And why not?

She hadn't been planning on keeping the baby, but she would settle into their life here.

She would be happy. And as for the truth…once

she was convinced of the rightness of all of this the truth wouldn't matter.

"And you swept me off my feet?" she asked.

"Something like that."

"No really," she said. "Tell me."

She was looking at him all open and sweet and he remembered her being much more guarded when they'd first met. She trusted him now. She wasn't looking at him like he was a predator set on devouring her.

He idly wondered if this was a moment another man might feel something like guilt.

"Your...friends ended up leaving early. It was raining. We were the only two people left at the ruins, and you came back home with me." It was impossible to keep his voice from growing huskier. Impossible to hide the rising desire inside of him because thinking of that night made him think of how it had been.

If he pushed through the memories of grief, if he ignored why he'd been there in the first place, he could remember the way her skin had felt beneath his hands. The way she'd looked up at him in wonder as she'd found her release...

"I did?"

"Yes."

"Then what?"

She looked so guileless, and if he didn't know for a fact she'd just woken up after being in a coma for a month he would have thought it was an act. Not that it couldn't be an act but he doubted she'd be that quick to slip into one.

No, whatever Riot was…he'd never thought her an actress.

A sorceress, perhaps, for no other woman had ever managed to get under his skin in quite so accomplished a fashion.

"Our connection was immediate," he said. "And physical."

She blinked. "No. Now I know you're lying. Sorry, there is no way I went back to your place and…no."

"No way?"

"None," she said, shaking her head.

"I hate to disappoint you, but you did. You had known me all of one hour when you took your clothes off for me."

She laughed at him. Sleeping Beauty had the audacity to laugh at him. "It didn't happen that way. I'm a virgin."

Then she seemed to remember herself, putting her hand over her mouth, color suffusing her cheeks. "I don't know why I said that. I don't know why I'm talking to you like this except you say I know you, and now you're telling me I slept with you moments after meeting you and I'm sorry I just…can't make that make sense. Not when I know what I know about the rest of my life."

"But you don't know anything about the days leading up to your trip. Or what happened on it," he pointed out.

A virgin?

Was it possible?

She wasn't one now, that was for certain. But it had never once occurred to him that the sensual woman he'd taken into his arms that night had never been with another man.

"I guess I had a whole personality transplant. Believe me, I'm not adventurous. I…"

Something else changed in her face just then and it galled him that even now he couldn't read this woman. Even now she was a mystery to him.

Women were not mysteries in his world. They filled a very specific purpose, fed a specific appetite and then he didn't think of them again.

It was how people were in his world.

They outlived their usefulness, and then they were gone from it.

Now he had a baby, and practically speaking, babies served no use at all. But he would have her, forever.

And now there was Riot, and he was going to have her forever too.

And she mystified him.

"I must be adventurous," she whispered. "I must be. Because I went to Cambodia and I met you and we…we did, didn't we?" She seemed hypnotized then and his heart did something it had never done before.

He had no words for it.

An ache, a squeeze and a thunder all at once, as she leaned forward with a questioning look on her face. And she placed her hand on his chest. Over that muscle that was reacting to her even now.

Her eyes met his and the wonder he saw there mirrored what he'd seen when he'd entered her body that night they'd been together.

He curled his fingers around her wrist and felt everything begin to burn.

And then an ear-shattering wail split the silence. Riot went still. "What is that?"

CHAPTER FOUR

HER MIND WAS REELING. It had been blank when she'd woken up but now it was…it was overly full. With this place, with this man.

Engaged? It seemed impossible.

She couldn't remember anything, and she really had no idea how she had gone on her trip, a woman who had never been kissed, and ten months later found herself engaged to the most beautiful man she'd ever seen in her life.

Who was also obviously wealthy?

None of it made sense.

But she could feel something between them. Something like she'd never experienced before and she'd felt compelled to draw near to it.

But the crying baby had stopped everything.

"Where is the baby?" she asked, her heart thundering in desperation.

"It is not time to have that discussion."

Panic. Desperation. Terror.

"Why not?" she asked.

"Because it is not."

But she didn't listen. On her unsteady legs she got out of the bed and ran. She stumbled forward, her knee coming down hard on the carpet, which bit into her skin and she cursed the ridiculous nightgown she was still wearing.

The baby.

There was a baby.

She'd been asleep for a whole month.

She opened the door just as he reached for her, pulling her back against his hard body as it opened to reveal a woman standing there, holding a tiny little bundle, cradled to her chest.

The baby had dark hair, her skin golden. None of Riot was visible at all. She looked for her own features, desperately and didn't see any.

She saw *him*.

But there was nothing that decisively stated that she was there as well.

But she felt it. *She felt it,* and she couldn't say what it was.

She knew so little right now. She knew nothing about how she had gotten to this place in her life. And she didn't look at her fiancé and know anything.

But looking at this child, she knew.

"What's her name," she whispered, his hands still holding her in an iron grip.

"Soriya," he said.

It was a beautiful name and she wanted to ask what it meant, but that desire was overshadowed by her need to hold the baby. She was fussing and hic-cupping and the woman holding her might as well have been invisible because she didn't matter to Riot at all.

All she could see was Soriya.

"Give her to me," she demanded.

"There is explaining…"

"There is no explaining," she said, pulling out of his hold with Herculean effort. "The child is mine, I know she is."

"We do not wish to upset you," he said, his voice firm.

"Do not treat me like a child. This is my baby. Give her to me," she demanded in a voice she didn't entirely recognize. But the woman holding the baby—a nanny she assumed—immediately did as Riot said.

And then she placed the soft, warm bundle into her arms and the whole world seemed to change. Again.

She'd woken up in a life she didn't know. And this should be yet more confusion. But it wasn't.

It was all suddenly clear. Because while she didn't remember him. And she couldn't understand how she'd come to be engaged to him, and she really couldn't believe she'd chucked twenty-two years of virginity out the window in an afternoon, she could believe this.

This child.

She knew her, down in her bones, maybe because her body had knit her together. She knew her.

And the grief that overwhelmed her for a moment took her breath away.

She didn't remember falling in love.

She didn't remember the touch of his hands on her body.

She didn't remember carrying this baby, or telling him about the pregnancy. Was he happy? Had they been filled with joy? Did they have to move the wedding date up or…they must have decided to wait until after she was born.

And the birth…

She had missed all of it.

Had forgotten her stomach growing rounder by the week. Had slept through the labor pains. How could she have delivered while asleep?

It was too much to take in. She'd slept with this man. Had a relationship with him. Had his baby. All of it was gone.

Except…

It wasn't all gone.

This baby was hers, and whether it made sense that she knew it or not, she did.

She hadn't held her baby. The baby was a month old and she'd never held her.

Suddenly her chest felt like it was caving in on itself. It was all too overwhelming. She'd been awake for hours after the baby had been separated from her for so long and no one had brought her to Riot.

"Why didn't you bring her to me immediately?" she asked, angry that there had been hours where she could have been holding her child and hadn't been.

"Concern," he said, his voice hard. "It is difficult enough for you to believe all that passed between us. To lose this from your memory…"

"She is mine," she said.

"Yes."

"I know," she whispered. She did. She knew it with her whole heart. Her whole soul.

Suddenly everything felt terrifying and precarious. He knew so much more about her than she did, and the only good thing was that he must love her. No one else in her life ever had. But if he loved her, and he had taken care of her so it seemed that he must, he wouldn't do her any harm.

He wouldn't take Soriya from her.

And she suddenly felt desperately, horribly afraid. Not of this unprecedented situation that she found herself in, but that she might actually be asleep now. That this was a dream.

Because how had the girl that she had been when last she remembered, woken up to be engaged. Woken up to be the mother of this perfect, beautiful child. It didn't make any sense. She had never been lovely or compelling or desired.

Her own mother hadn't wanted anything to do with her at all, much less her father.

And somehow, she had managed to get herself into the situation where… Where she was different.

Where everything was different. It was like waking up in an entirely new life.

It wasn't like that, it *was* that. And she couldn't... She would never be able to...

And she realized she didn't even know his name.

"I'm sorry, we have not been properly introduced."

He looked at her, as if she had said something extremely surprising. And she supposed that she had. But she didn't know what was surprising right now. She felt at sea, and utterly ignorant of everything. And he knew everything. He knew about the baby. Everything about her. Riot didn't. She hadn't even known she was pregnant.

"Kravann," he said. "Valenti. If I had friends, they would call me Krav."

"Oh."

"Yes. It means nothing to you, I take it?"

"No. It just doesn't... None of this... I don't remember anything. I don't remember any of this. I don't remember you. But then... I'm not entirely certain that I remember myself. Because I just... I am not interesting enough to have met you and gone back to your place and..." She realized that she was still speaking in front of the nanny.

And then he gestured to the woman. "Leave us."

Riot took the baby in her arms, holding her close. She was so warm and weighty. She wanted to cling to her forever. She had never felt anything like this, the strange sense of peace that stole over her even in the midst of all this turmoil. And if there was one thing she knew right now it was that this child was hers. Regardless of whether or not she remembered it. This child was hers.

"We will find our way," he said.

And she wondered if he had been worried about her. If he had been keeping a bedside vigil. It was difficult to imagine this man worried. He was... She had never known a man like him, that was certain. Her experience with men was limited, it was true. But even so, she felt that he was the sort of man that wasn't common in the least.

He had an air of authority about him that was entirely different from any other person she'd known.

And all of this...

"I just have so many questions," she said. "I feel like I need to... Piece together the whole last ten months immediately."

"You do not have to," he said. "We have the rest of our lives, Riot. The rest of our lives to determine who we are. You do not need to put yourself back together in five minutes. Head injuries are complex, so I have been told many times over the last month."

"Can you start with telling me what... What happened to me?"

"No. I think we should start with getting you moved to a better room. I think we should start with you getting cleaned up, and then having dinner."

She was in a nightgown, and she couldn't deny that there was likely some validity to what he was saying, but that would require that she separate from Soriya.

She held the baby closer.

"She has been with me this last month. She will be fine with me for a few moments more."

He took out his phone, and opened something, pushing a button inside of the app. And moments later, two members of staff she had not yet seen appeared.

"Yes, Mr. Valenti?"

"Please take my fiancée to her room. She will be in different quarters now. Help her select an outfit for dinner. Show her to the bathroom and draw her a bath."

"Yes sir."

And with that, Riot found herself being ushered away from Soriya, and from Krav, and she felt like the world had been upended yet again.

They were her anchors, she realized, even though she couldn't remember either of them.

Because this whole world was foreign, but if it was Krav's world, then she could at least work out why she was in it.

It didn't take any imagination at all to see why she would've been tempted to go with him.

"Is he… He always like this?" she asked.

"Always like what, miss?" one of the women asked her.

"He's quite… Autocratic."

"I found him to be quite soft in that moment," the other woman said. "Typically he is…"

"He growls like a tiger," the other finished.

And they smiled at each other. A burning sensation of jealousy sparked in Riot's stomach. And she knew that was silly. How could she be jealous over a man she didn't even know? Anyway, they were engaged. In theory.

The entire house was grand, and she had barely had a chance to take it in, but when she was ushered into the room that was to be hers, the breath was stolen entirely out of her lungs.

It was…

It was so different than the rather intense, Gothic appearance of the rest of the manor.

It was light. White with soft pink accents everywhere. The bed was like a cloud. All white and cotton fluffy pink with gold for the poster frame and gauzy netting wrapped around it.

It was so open and airy, so different from the room she had just come from. So different from… From anything she had ever seen before, and yet somehow it was perfectly what she would've chosen for herself.

Was it strange, though, that there was this room here prepared for her and they didn't share it?

She wondered if that was just how rich people did things. She knew that royalty often had separate bedrooms. Maybe it was… Maybe it was something the wealthy tended to do. She wouldn't know.

She hadn't known any wealthy people, not in her whole life. And he was clearly...

She tried so hard to remember. She tried so hard to cast her mind back.

Really, it was no mystery how he could've gotten her to let her guard down. He was the most beautiful man she had ever seen. And she might've thought that she wouldn't have very many chances like that in her life. To sleep with a man who was quite that beautiful.

How horribly inconvenient that she was no longer a virgin and she couldn't even remember having sex.

Of all the things to be upset about, that was perhaps a very silly one, but she did feel upset about it in the moment.

"What would you like to wear?"

One woman went over to a vast, ornate wardrobe and threw the doors open. And inside was the most delicious array of clothing Riot had ever seen.

Organized by the colors of the rainbow, deep jewel tones and pops of bright color dazzled her. It was like a dream. She didn't like to admit it, but the fact of the matter was she was a magpie. She loved beautiful things. It was only that she had been able to own very few of them.

Her home back in Georgia was a small collection of curated things that she had saved up for, that she loved.

Because when she could buy something nice, she savored it. And now there was this entire room full of delicious things. All gifts, and there was something that made her feel breathless in that.

But then, for him, these gifts must come so easy. For her, everything beautiful had always represented hours of work. It had to have great value to her, because if it didn't, why would she put in so much work in order to have it. Money that went out had been painstakingly saved.

And she couldn't decide if it meant more or less that it had come from him.

Maybe it doesn't matter. Maybe you're just trying to attach meaning to things because you can't find an anchor.

Now that could be very well true.

She needed to get back to him. She needed to get back to Soriya.

"Mr. Valenti will want you ready in the next hour. That is when he eats dinner."

"He eats dinner at the same time every night?"

One of the women nodded. "Yes. He does. He is a man of exacting schedule."

That didn't surprise her. He seemed… Exacting. And she was hungry for details about him. Because he was apparently a singular man in her life. A sea change in a suit. And she knew nothing about him.

There were things about him she could not quite… *grasp.* Her mind was desperately trying to fill in all of these blanks, but if she did not know that he was her fiancé she would've said that he… He did not seem like a man with a great well of emotion inside of him. There was something hard and dark about him. Something that felt quite dangerous. But that wasn't the kind of person that she was drawn to. It never had been.

She had never quite understood the appeal of the bad boy. In theory, she had decided that she liked nice men.

Of course, she had never got around to dating one. Because any man who proclaimed to be nice never was. And as far as nice men went… That was all she had ever found.

And for some reason, she chose a dress that was the color of a peacock, all shimmery and rich, and then allowed herself to be led to the bathroom where she found a deep tub that they filled with warm, scented water. Flowers were scattered over the surface, and a silk robe left out for her. And then she was left to her own devices.

She sank slowly into the water, and sighed. One thing she did know was that it had been a very long time since she'd taken a bath.

She couldn't believe that she was missing all of this time in her memory. It didn't seem possible. That so much of life had just…evaporated. The part that she had forgotten, and the part that she had been asleep through.

Asleep.

No. She hadn't been asleep. Obviously, she had been in an accident. But she didn't even know the details about that.

She tried to push it to the back of her mind, slowly beginning to wash herself. But her mind went back to Krav.

And as she moved her fingertips over her own skin, it was far too easy to imagine that the hands were his.

An electric shock went through her body.

How could she be thinking about… That? How could that be the leading thing that she… Well, if what he'd said was true about their meeting, that had been their first connection. And while she couldn't quite imagine it, maybe that was… Maybe that was the key.

She had met him, and apparently, she had been overcome by the chemistry between them. She could feel it even now.

Even with all of this… Even with so many bigger, grander things at stake… She was thinking about things that had never concerned her prior to meeting him.

She got out of the bath, swathing herself in the silk robe, and looking in the mirror. Her eyes were bright, her skin pink. She looked a bit sallow, beneath the color that had been brought on by the bath, and she let the robe fall away, examining her body in the mirror. She looked at her stomach, and tears filled her eyes. Stretch marks. A bit of extra skin.

A scar where the child had been delivered…

So that was how she'd had the baby when she'd been asleep.

Tears filled her eyes.

She had carried a baby. A *child*. And she couldn't remember...

There was a firm knock on the door. "Miss?"

And after that, there was no time to be standing there feeling sorry for herself in front of a mirror. She was hurriedly dressed and her hair brushed. Makeup applied to her face, and when she looked back in the mirror, she was yet again staring at a stranger, but not for the same reasons.

She made her way from the room, led by her entourage to the dining room.

And there he was, standing at the head of the table, wearing a dark suit. The room was vast, ornate, and heavy like the other room she had been in was. Not like that stunning bright bedroom of hers.

There was something old money about this. Something dark.

"There you are," he said.

But there was a weight beneath the words that set off a fire in her stomach.

"Yes. Is Soriya here..."

"She is down for her nap. She often takes a small nap just at this time then wakes again for a snack before going down for the night."

She couldn't deny she was disappointed by that. But suddenly she was ravenous. And her hunger overtook everything else.

Dinner was beautiful. And for a moment, she forgot about all the things she had forgotten. For a moment, she allowed herself to believe that her last memory was yesterday, and today she was standing in this beautiful, palatial home with the most glorious spread of food in front of her that she had ever seen.

For a moment, she allowed herself to believe that her life had simply transformed in an instant.

And she felt like…not like a sad, confused girl, but for the first time like perhaps she was a secret princess.

The idea made her eyes sting.

She had seen a movie when she was a teenager all about that. About a girl whose long absent father was secretly a king.

And she, secretly a princess. And sometimes, Riot had wished that was her life. That she was royalty. And someday somebody would come and take her away from her mother and give her a completely different life.

Instead, she carved out a life for herself, once she had accepted that fairy tales weren't real.

But now she felt like she was in one, and just for a moment, she wanted to embrace it. Wanted to feel it.

"Have a seat," he said.

She did as she was told, taking a seat in the chair across from him.

Being this close to him… He was even more beautiful than she had realized.

"You are…remarkable," he said. "I should imagine that most people who have gone through the ordeal you have do not come out of it looking half so well."

"I bet there aren't very many people who have gone through what I have," she said. "This seems more like a soap opera than real life."

"I told myself that quite a few times while you lay there. It was... A low point."

"For you?"

"I'm the kind of man who believes that he could fix anything. But I could not fix you. I brought in the best medical help that I could. But I was told that nothing but time would wake you. If you woke at all."

She hadn't considered that. That she might never have woken. She would never have known about Soriya. Would never have remembered Krav.

What if she had woken but years later? Missing so much time...

It made her chest burn.

"But I did wake up," she said fiercely.

"Yes," he said. "You did."

"I don't know where to begin."

"We will be married as soon as possible," he said.

But something in her jumped in fear. "I don't even remember you."

"It does not matter. We are a family. And we have waited all this time to be so. You shall be my bride."

"A bride who doesn't know her husband?"

He looked at her, his dark eyes serious, compelling. "I seduced you once. I have no problem doing it again."

And she shivered. Because the very idea of a man like him turning his focus to…seducing her… It made her…

Well, her body sang with the possibilities.

"I want to know about you," she said. "I don't remember anything. I'm sure we already did all the boring getting to know you sort of things, but…"

"My father was very wealthy. As was his father. As was his. I think you understand where this is going. The Valentis are very old Italian family."

"Right."

"The empire has expanded. We own a great many hotels. There is also a manufacturing arm. Property development. There is very little that we do not have our hands in. I am as financially secure as a person can be."

"I don't… I don't even understand that. I've never been financially secure a day in my life."

"You are now," he said. "You have nothing to worry about. All of your needs will be met with me. All of Soriya's needs will be met."

That rubbed against something wounded in her soul.

Her mother had resented her so much, and a huge part of that had been because of the financial instability they found themselves in. At least, that was what Riot told herself. The alternative was that she just wasn't lovable. That no matter what, her mother wouldn't have cared. So, she liked to excuse her on the basis of stress and fear. Because it made things easier.

Why couldn't she have forgotten that, but remembered him? This man who was beautiful and offering to take care of her.

Why was so much of him a blank space?

"How did we fall in love?"

He leaned back in his chair, his elbow resting on the arm of it, his dark eyes fathomless. Compelling.

"I told you how we met. It was undeniable. This thing between us."

"It must've been. Otherwise, I never would have… I was raised my whole life to be very cautious about strangers. And particularly strange men. I built up a pretty healthy immunity to them. So, I can't imagine that encountering you alone in a ruin would've made me feel altogether very confident."

"You were not," he said. "You were skittish at first. But you needed a ride. I brought you back. You didn't leave."

"And then what happened?"

She was looking up at him with expectation. Her breath coming in short, sharp bursts, her eyes wide. She was greatly anticipating the story he was about to tell, and up until this moment, everything he'd said had been true.

Krav had never considered himself a liar. But he had never worried over much about it either. If a lie would do better than the truth, there was no harm in it as far as he was concerned. And he had decided before she had come out to dinner that he had one goal. To make her his bride. To make this thing between them last.

He could not be the sole parent in Soriya's life. It would be a mistake. Beyond a mistake. He had vague memories of the way his mother had held him. Of the way she had taken care of him. But vague memories were all he had.

The things that he remembered with sharp clarity were the harsh beatings that his father had doled out. The cruelty. The way that he had belittled him. And he would never...

He would never do that to Soriya. He was not afraid of being his father.

But there was a gray space that he feared almost more.

He was a man who prided himself on being an expert in all things. But he was not an expert on how to care for a child. How to give them what they needed.

And he feared his negligence would cause irreparable damage.

He was a cold bastard.

And that was why lying now seemed easy.

There was no reason not to.

She wanted a love story.

He thought of their days together. The nights. If he had been another man, that would have been a romance. But of course, he had shattered the illusion in the end.

He could see that she needed a love story. So why not give it to her? Why not give her the love story that she needed to be happy?

Maybe somewhere in there he would find that space again.

Where she had looked at him with joy and he had felt...

The days had stretched on there, like endless summer days he'd heard about but never had. The Valenti heir could never be still. Could never take a break. Could never rest.

With her, sometimes it had felt like rest.

He had tricked her into seeing a man, and not the monster he knew he was.

He wanted that again.

She needs it, that's what matters.

"It was like you had always been there," he said.

"I cooked for you. We stayed at the tree house for a while after. Then we moved on to my hotel in the city. From there we went back to Europe. We took a tour."

"I must've gotten pregnant very quickly," she said.

"Yes," he said. "Though, we...were often overcome with passion."

Her cheeks went scarlet, and he wanted to touch her. "What happened? When I found out?"

"You were scared," he said. Because she must've been. Then again, he felt that it was best if there was a ring of truth to all of this.

He saw that moment again in his mind.

I'm pregnant.

She had been happy.

He had taken that happiness and crushed it in his fist.

He had thought…

But what if it had gone differently?

He took his mind back there, to that moment.

For one moment, it was like he was there, at that dinner. Looking at her in that stunning dress as she said those words to him again.

I'm pregnant.

And this time, he made a new choice. The Krav in his vision changed.

He made a new story.

"But I told you… I told you not to worry. I told you that we would be in this together." And he could see it, in his mind. It was the strangest thing. He could imagine holding her against him, taking hold of her chin and tilting her face upward. Kissing away her tears. In this story, he was a man he had never been. One who knew how to be tender if it was required.

"Have you been married before?"

"No," he said.

"But you were ready to marry me?"

"Yes," he said. "I was… I don't have any other children, either. I did not plan on becoming a father. But once I found out… There was never any question of what I would do."

And that again was true.

"Oh." And she began to cry.

"Why are you crying?"

"Because… You say that as if…as if fathers just take care of their children. As if a man would obviously take care of the woman whose baby she's having. But…that has not been my life. My father wanted nothing to do with me, my own mother didn't care for me. And that I remember. But I can't remember you… I can't remember us. And it breaks my heart. Because I wish so much I could remember that moment. I bet it was the best moment of my life."

And he hardened his heart, into stone. Into obsidian, because he could not afford to be moved by this.

Hell, he had never in his life had to try to not be moved by anything. Except for her beauty. Her beauty was…

It had been the thing that had gotten in and undermined his control in the beginning. And it hadn't changed much now.

"We will put it back together. That I promise you. And then… You will know that you should be my bride. My wife."

"Thank you," she said.

"Knowing that we are in love. Knowing that you love me… It's the greatest gift I could've ever asked for."

And he knew that meant he must show her the truth of it as best he could.

He must weave together a story that was so compelling she could never find the lie. She would never want to. If she knew the man he was, she would not feel this way.

If she knew his flaws. His darkness.

She would run away again, as she had that night.

He would have to hope that she did not remember the truth.

CHAPTER FIVE

RIOT HAD BEEN afraid to go to sleep that night. She had been asked to be taken to Soriya's room, and there she had stayed. She had held her baby, gazing down at her and trying to understand how her life had taken such a strange new shape so quickly.

And then she had simply rocked her, held her. She had very little memory of going to bed. But when she woke up that morning, cocooned in impossible softness, she was nearly afraid to open her eyes. If she did, would she be gone? Would her baby be gone?

Would she wake up and find that she was actually just still Riot, sad and alone in Georgia having had no adventures, and no life-changing loves?

But she opened her eyes and saw that pink canopy cloud, and she breathed a sigh of relief.

She would take not remembering if she was able to wake up here. She would take it every day if she had to.

Krav was nowhere to be found that morning, so she went and got Soriya out of bed, and played with her. She was so…she was so happy with how easily her daughter took to her.

She found herself weeping often throughout the day, and she wondered if there was a time when she wouldn't feel overwhelmed by emotion over the situation. But she didn't mind. Not now.

"He brought her to see you every day."

She was getting assistance from the nanny still, it was helpful, and she didn't want to take a steady caregiver away from Soriya while she was still getting used to Riot.

It hurt. It hurt to realize that this other woman had spent more time with her baby than she had.

But she was a soft, grandmotherly figure, and as long as Riot thought of her that way, it settled all right.

Particularly since her own mother would never make a good grandmother to Soriya.

She wondered about Krav's mother. Wondered if she was still alive. If Soriya would have any grandparents…

"He did?"

"Yes. It was very important to him that she knew you."

She was touched by that.

Later, they went outside and she laid out a blanket for Soriya, and the nanny left the two of them alone to simply enjoy their time together.

She smiled as she watched her little girl crawl around, from the blanket to the grass.

And she looked up at the blue sky and wondered how she had gotten quite so lucky.

It was still like a dream, but over the next few days she woke up every morning and it seemed to remain.

She made going and lying on the lawn with Soriya a routine. And it was wonderful. If there was anything that settled uneasily in her it was her relationship with Krav. She couldn't quite… She couldn't quite square up the way that she felt around him with the fact that they were supposed to be in love. There was attention there. Something that she couldn't quite readily define. He was so kind. And incredibly patient.

But her afternoons were happiest when it was just her and Soriya. Because at least there everything seemed simple.

She stared up at the sky, her beautiful child next to her, and for the first time, things in her life felt…

Perfect.

Krav watched her from his position on the balcony. He pressed his hands firmly into the marble as he gazed down at her below.

The sight of her with the child made him feel an intense sense of possessiveness.

That he had nearly lost them both seemed unconscionable now.

But they were here. They were here and they were his. And it was time. She had been awake for a week, and he had kept a respectable distance. Trying to gauge exactly what was happening with her memory.

It seemed to him—Doctor though he was not—that there was no point waiting around to see if it might return. She was happy. He would do his best to make her his.

And once those things were accomplished, there would be no question about her remaining with him. With Soriya.

It was what she wanted, after all. Or had been. He was not a man given to self reflection, but he knew that he had reacted...badly. He was not a man given to regret either, but it had been a constant gnawing regret ever since.

But now she was back. And it was his chance to rewrite what had occurred before.

He would not question the gift.

For months he had lived in a darkness he couldn't get through.

That he had taken this beautiful creature and shattered her.

That he had caused the loss of her child.

Their child.

It hit him now, harder than ever, for that child was Soriya, not merely a possibility but a human being, so small and helpless and dependent.

This new story...

Riot was here, Soriya was here.

He didn't have to go back to that moment.

He walked down the curved staircase onto the

grass below, and went to stand before Riot, whose blond hair was spread out all around her like a halo. She sat up, her cheeks turning pink, and he felt an answering desire echo in his stomach. No matter how many times he had had her, he had never been able to satiate the need that he felt for her.

She was too beautiful. Too perfect.

And the way that she fit in his arms, the magic that they created between their bodies, it was more than simple sex, and always had been.

He had been on the verge of sending her away before she had found out she was pregnant.

Because the heat between them wasn't dying down, it only seemed to be growing more intense, and he did not have a place for that in his life.

He was not a man who did permanent. Or even close.

And now here he was, bound and determined to make this forever.

But if there was one thing he would not do, it was repeat the sins of his father.

He very nearly had. Perhaps not in the sense that he had done the exact things his father had done to his mother, but in the sense that he had failed. Failed his child. Failed the woman who was bearing that child.

He would not fail them again.

"I rarely see you during the day," she said, sitting up and pushing her hair off her forehead.

She was such a lovely, delicate thing.

She scooped Soriya up from the blanket and held her close to her breast.

"I was looking for you."

"We come out here every day," Riot said, smiling. "She loves to be outside."

"Good. She has not been away from the estate yet. That is what I wish to speak to you about. We have not…that is…our relationship was private. As was your pregnancy. And given the circumstances surrounding Soriya's birth…nobody knows that she was born. And no one knows that you are part of my life."

"And it will matter," she said softly. "Because you are part of such an old family."

That wasn't even the half of it. He was one of the richest men in the world. And the media hounded him like they would a movie star.

Perhaps even more so, because he was so private. So, he was a point of interest. Somewhat unknowable.

"There will be interest in the fact that I'm getting married. There will be interest in the fact that I've had a child. I could send an announcement out to the media, but I do wonder if it would perhaps be best if we were just…seen together."

"What was it like before?"

He hesitated. "We… We kept a low profile. After you and I were together in Cambodia. We traveled, a bit. But we stayed away from Rome and other major cities. We went to the Amalfi Coast." He watched her face. Watched to see if that jogged any sort of memory. He hoped it did not.

"I see."

"It is fairly easy to keep away from prying eyes in those places. And I have many residences."

"Was I your dirty secret?"

She had been. But not because of the things they did together. Because of the things that she made him feel. He thought nothing of trotting out mistresses to the public. But he had felt protective of her from the beginning. And the thing between them had not felt common or indeed like anything he felt like sharing with the public.

He had not felt like sharing her.

He had shown her something in him he had hidden all his life, that night after his mother's funeral. He had let her see him.

He had raised his barriers again after that, but he had...

He had felt the need to hide her, to hide them, to draw a curtain around them and keep that weakness she'd brought out in him a secret.

"So what exactly are you proposing?"

"That we go out. As a family."

The smile that lit up her face felt like a stick of dynamite going off in his chest. "Yes, please. I would like that."

"You're feeling up to it?"

"I feel fine. Other than the fact that I cannot remember what has to have been the most significant year of my life, I feel wonderful. I've never been so happy."

Krav brooded on that as they got ready to go into the city. She was still living in his house, but they were not sharing space. It was entirely different from when they had been in the midst of their affair.

She had often spent whole days naked in his villas. He would dismiss the staff for the week so that she could lounge by the pool and do nothing and he could come home from work to ravish her.

She had been all he wanted.

And he had certainly not thought of living with her when sex was not the primary objective.

How things had changed.

Though his desire for her had not. When she came down the stairs wearing a white dress that skimmed over her curves in an easy manner, and fell to her knees, his breath took a leave of absence.

And then there was the way she cradled the child...

"Would you like to hold her?"

"No," he said.

Her smile faltered. "I don't mind."

"You missed the first month of her life. Hold her."

"Okay," she returned, keeping the child cradled to her breast.

He extended his arm, and the two of them walked out the front door, to the limousine that was waiting for them.

"This seems... I can't even believe this," she said.

She fussed around buckling Soriya in her car seat, and then looked at him, as if seeking reassurance.

"All looks well," he said.

Typically, the nannies did this. He did not…hold her.

She was tiny and frail and he…

He broke things that were fragile.

"Good," she said.

She slid into the limo, and looked around, her eyes wide.

"We will be going to one of my favorite restaurants."

"Did we do this a lot?"

"Sometimes. I often like to keep you at home to myself."

The innocence in her expression nearly undid him.

It reminded him of when they had first met. By the end of everything, she had learned what he liked.

She had become accomplished at pleasing him, and any embarrassment she seemed to have about things of a sexual nature had vanished.

It was fascinating to see a return to who she had been before.

"Why?"

He chuckled. He did not know if this was the time to bring up the physical connection between the two of them.

What he wanted was to build the scaffolding for something that would be strong.

He had the chance to change the truth. And why wouldn't he?

Why wouldn't he?

"I like to have you to myself," he said. "Then when my desire for you overtook everything else... There were no barriers."

It had been a calculated risk, but it had been the right one. Because whatever she remembered or didn't, this remained between them. This fire, this heat. It was why they were in the situation in the first place. The unrelenting chemistry between the two of them transcended everything that Krav had ever known.

He was a man who had known many women.

He was expert in pleasing them and walking away having felt nothing but release.

What had burned between them had always been something undeniable, something else entirely. And he had told himself for a long time it was because of when they met. Because he had been diminished since his mother's death.

But now it felt like perhaps that was far too simple a truth.

Now it felt like perhaps there was more. Like there had to be.

She seemed pleased by that.

"I just wish that I could remember..."

"Perhaps it is not a matter of remembering. Only discovering."

He remembered. He remembered everything perfectly. Up until the bitter end when it had all exploded.

When you destroyed it.

It had been necessary, or rather it had felt so at the time.

But now...

Now here she was again. All of them together.

"Maybe," she said. "I've been trying to wrap my head around the fact that I'm a mother. It's difficult for me to see where you fit in."

"Let me show you."

And he had never wanted to be gentle with someone in all of his life, but he wanted to be gentle with her. Right now, he wanted to learn to do things and be things that he had never once desired to be.

Right now, he wanted to be the man that he had needed to be when she had told him she was having a child. The man he had been unable to be. He had months to sit with that. To sit with the loss of the pregnancy. And then the miracle of finding out she hadn't lost the child after all. Then the uncertainty of her own health.

And then she had woken up remembering nothing. It gave him a chance to change it all.

The restaurant was open-air, right out on the street where they could easily be seen. And it was his favorite. Not because of that, but because of how amazing the food was.

Whenever they had shared a meal together, she had always enjoyed it. But he had spent that time willing her to finish, so that they could get down to what he truly wanted. Which was always stripping her out of whatever she was wearing and being inside of her again.

It wasn't that he didn't want it now. But there was something about the moment that he didn't mind lingering in. Something about the moment itself that seemed like enough.

And it allowed him to truly watch her as she ate her food. As she delighted in it.

"I have never had anything so amazing."

She had always enjoyed the food when he had taken her out, and it hadn't occurred to him that she didn't remember any of those meals.

"You have," he said. "You just don't recall. I fed you well during our time together."

She laughed. "Well, there is something to be said for getting to discover this all over again. If I can have some humor about it."

Their eyes caught and held, and desire arced between them. There was no denying it.

"Maybe there will be something to be said for discovering other things for the first time all over again."

"Though, by your very admission, your first time with me was your… Your first time."

"I didn't tell you?" she asked.

"No. You didn't. We never spoke of the past. Past lovers, I mean. You told me only small details about your life."

"Well, the story of my past life is only sad."

"I do not think you are sad."

A small smile curved her lips. "That is something."

"I'm glad you think so."

"And what about you? Did we talk about… Your past?"

"I'm much more interested in my potential future. With you."

She let out a satisfied sigh, and then a chocolate cake was put in front of her and she grinned brightly.

"I'm sorry that we didn't attract any media attention," she said.

"What are you talking about?" he said. "We've been having our picture taken this entire time."

Her eyes widened. "We have? How did I not realize?"

"You aren't used to it. But I am. The thing about the paparazzi now is that the ability to take photos is on your phone. They're able to be much more subtle when the mood strikes. Oftentimes they still like a telephoto lens and gross invasions of privacy, or sticking a camera in your face. Though, they do not enjoy doing that with me so much."

"Why?"

He smiled. "They're afraid of me."

She shivered, her shoulders twitching back and forth.

"What?" he asked.

"Sometimes I sense that about you."

"What?"

"That you are to be feared. That you are… A predator." She laughed. "I don't know why I think that.

I realized as soon as I said it how silly it sounded. Because you've been nothing but wonderful this entire time. It's just that…"

A disquiet grip took hold of him. She could see it. The darkness in him. And he had let it out, the full weight of it when she had told him about her pregnancy, and she didn't even remember that, and still she knew.

But he would not unleash it on her again.

He had broken her, and he had nearly ruined all of this. More months, he'd been sure he had. He had kept watch on her through his people and yet never allowed himself to look in on her, not even once.

Had never allowed himself to directly ask about her.

Because he had not deserved to see her.

Not after the way he'd sinned against her.

But now…now things were different. He was making it so.

There would be a way to do this. She would be his wife. They would share a bed.

She would believe that he was in love with her. And that would be enough.

She would care for the child…

All would be well.

"Well, I'm glad that you realize I'm not one."

"Of course not," she said. "You're just a very handsome man."

It was such a sweet, but new sort of complement

that it caught him off guard. Touched him in places he did not expect.

"Handsome?"

"Well, it's nicer than dangerous, isn't it?"

"Indeed," he said.

"Come," he said when they finished. "Let us walk."

They had an expensive pram for Soriya, and Riot pushed it, marveling at the city around them. She had never seen Rome before. At least, he assumed so given everything he knew about her.

And they had never come here together.

"This really is your first time here," he said.

A wave of relief seemed to move through her body. "That is actually good to know. It is unsettling. Not knowing what I don't remember, and what I actually haven't done."

"Yes. I can see that."

"I'm happy to be here with you. Really doing this for the first time."

And even while she was pushing the pram, she let go of the handle, and wrapped her fingers around his. They had never held hands.

Not even when they were at the peak of this thing between them.

Holding hands was…domestic. They had never been domestic.

But here they were, with a child, strolling down the street like they might've been…normal. And it would make for exactly the sort of picture he had been trying to have taken, but for some reason he could not bear it.

Slowly, he withdrew his hand from hers, and he could feel a slight withdrawal coming from within her, but she said nothing.

"I have made an appointment for us," he said.

"An appointment?"

And then he ushered her into the shop that was open only for them.

Her eyes widened when she looked around and saw all of the dresses hanging on the racks. Dresses that would fit her. He knew well how to shop for Riot's body already, and he had taken that knowledge and sent it ahead to the designer.

"Since we are to be married. I thought it would be a good idea for you to begin the selection process for your gown. You can have semicustom of course, but all of these are available, and can be altered in any way."

"I've never... I've never seen anything like this. And there's no way... You can't..."

"I'm a billionaire. I can do whatever I want. We could buy a plane and fly to space today if you wish. But I had thought we might start small. And with something that we actually need."

"A wedding gown. I..."

And then she started to do something truly distressing. She began to cry.

And he didn't know what to do. He simply stood there, frozen. And he was not a man who did loose

ends. He wasn't a man who did uncertainty. How did
this woman continually put him in a position where
he had no idea how he was supposed to react?

He had said nothing hurtful.

And she was weeping. Like a child.

"I'm sorry," she said. "It's only that… No one
has ever done so many nice things for me. And I am
so heartbroken that I don't remember meeting you.
I think you changed everything. You did. I woke
up from a coma and now I feel like I'm in a dream.
You have given me…" And then she launched herself into his arms, her face pressed against his chest,
and he could feel the moisture from her tears seep-
ing through his shirt.

And he felt… He was on fire. He had not held her
softness in his arms like this for nearly a year. This
woman… This woman who had come into his life
and upended everything… He had to watch her lie
in that bed motionless for a month. He had her out
of his life for eight months. It had been…torture. All
of it, but this was no better. This was…

This was like nothing he had ever experienced
before, and what he truly wanted to do was crush
his mouth to hers and show her how things really
were between them.

The intensity and the need. And do something
to rid himself of the yawning ache at the center of
his chest.

But he could only hold her.

"I'm sorry," she said, wiping at the tears on her face.

"It was just so unexpected. You know my mother always treated me like an imposition." She looked down at the pram. "I will never do that to her."

Conviction took hold of him. And while he didn't share anything about his father, his life, he wanted to share now.

And why not? In this new moment, when he was not the same man who she had run from that rainy night. But when he was the man who had heard of her pregnancy and reacted with joy. The man who had taken her into his arms and kissed her, who had proposed.

The man of the lie. Not the man he was in truth.

"My father treated me like his thing. I was nothing more than the heir to his fortune. He did not love me. He loved nothing but himself. And that would've been fine if he had the decency to have someone in my life who did love me." And he ignored the parallels between himself and his father right then. Ignored the reality of his relationship—or lack thereof—with his daughter.

He did not hold her. He had not. But he was doing the right thing. His father had wrenched him from the arms of someone who had loved him and brought him to a place where he had felt like nothing more than an obligation.

He would not do the same.

Her face was close to his, and it would be the easiest thing to grip her chin and hold her steady while he tasted her.

But if he kissed her once, he would not stop there.

He did not understand how to do a slow seduction. Not with her.

It was the softening that seemed to be required, that was what was so difficult. He wanted to drag her into the sitting room and have her. Show her why they had made this child. Why she was here. Why he could not forget her.

But she had forgotten him.

It struck him then, the hilarity of it.

For he had forgotten any number of women to pass through his bed, and they were always trying to win him back.

But this one. The biggest regret of his life. The one who had taken everything and turned it on its head, she had gone and forgotten him.

He supposed it was poetic justice in a way.

He would laugh, if it did not make his insides feel like they had been lit on fire.

She separated herself from him when the designer walked into the room. And she wiped the tears from her cheeks, and he wished that he would've done that instead.

It was a strange desire. One he barely recognized.

Soriya slept while Riot tried on different gowns, her beautiful figure swathed in silks and satins. And he simply sat and watched, the fire that had been banked for weeks now beginning to flare bright inside of him.

"I thought it was bad luck for the groom to see the bride before the wedding," she said.

"I think we had our share of bad luck already, don't you?"

She smiled. And then disappeared into the changing room again.

The problem with every dress that she tried on was that all he wanted to do was take them off of her. He had never imagined having a wife. And now... He was being bombarded with imagery that made it extremely clear that he was going to have a wife.

He already had a child.

He clenched his teeth together, tight.

"We will take three," he said. "The first, the fourth, and the last one."

"I don't get to choose?"

"Did you want to?"

"I'm... Somewhat angry that you chose my three favorites."

"Good," he said. "We have proven as compatible as ever. Memories or not."

"Why three?"

"You can choose whatever feels right on the day."

"That seems extreme. Maybe we should have gotten the spaceship."

"Don't be silly. They will be marginally less expensive than a spaceship."

"I guess so."

"Anyway. Billionaires launching themselves into

space is so done these days. Three wedding dresses is slightly more avant-garde."

She laughed. And it delighted him. There was no other word for it. He could not think of another thing that had delighted him, not since her. Not since every moment he had spent with her all those months ago.

And he was fascinated, that the man he'd become in this storybook romance he was writing could feel delight. Could laugh. Could make her laugh.

They wrapped the dresses up, and soon they were headed back to the estate. She let her head rest against the seat, her eyes resting on Soriya. "This was the best evening. Thank you. I feel... I'm not even sure I need to remember." She sighed heavily. "Like you said. Maybe it's more a matter of discovery."

And that was when he was determined. Determined to give her something good to discover. A new story.

She had not mentioned a ring, but surely she would notice soon enough that she didn't have one. He would give her what she should have had. When she told him she was pregnant she should have had a proposal. A ring. And he would give her that now.

Give her a romantic escape. Give her a reason to ground herself in this life. To discover that she wanted nothing more than to be with him. Then to be with Soriya.

Because he could remember all too clearly the woman he had devastated. The way that she had tripped and fallen and bled. The way that she had been gone from him, and he had been certain that he had…that he had destroyed her.

He wanted there to be something else in place of that. Even for him.

He would prepare the grandest proposal that there could be. And he would give her everything a woman could ever want.

In that he was determined.

CHAPTER SIX

SHE WAS STILL floating the next day. She felt like a high school girl with a crush. At least, she thought that might be what she felt like. It was still so strange, suspended in this bubble that didn't even feel like reality. Even going out into Rome hadn't made any of this feel more real. There was just something so… strange about it. And she wanted to believe it. She really did. He had bought her those gowns…

You don't have a ring.

She had noticed that. But there were many reasons that she might not have a ring.

She had never asked him about the accident she was in either. Was he in it too? It was weird that she didn't know.

She would talk to him about it. Last night, she had actually spent some time with him, and it had been nice.

She could imagine being his wife. She didn't think she had ever really spent that much time imagining what it would be like to be married. She had just sort of excluded that from her potential future. But she could imagine marrying Krav. If there was such a thing as a perfect man he might well be it.

Soriya was definitely the perfect baby. She had little experience with children, but she was loving all of this.

She was starting to feel a little bit more grounded when Krav walked into the dining room that morning and announced that they would be going to Paris. And that was disconnected from any reality that she had ever known. "Have I been to Paris?" she asked, which she realized was a strange question.

"No," he said.

"Well, I'm glad of that. I would hate for my first time in Paris to be lost in the mists of my mind."

She hated everything that was lost in the mists. She wished that she could remember...

But there was no point being upset about that. Not really.

She was taken care of. He was taking her to Paris, after all.

Her stomach fluttered.

She wondered when the physical part of their relationship would...when it would begin again.

She had spoken to her doctor, and she knew that she was technically still recovering from giving birth.

Or rather, had been until recently. She was no longer bleeding, and she wasn't sore in any way.

She had been told that meant she could return to...
regular intercourse.

Something that seemed kind of hilarious to her
because she couldn't remember having intercourse
of any kind.

It was the private jet that succeeded in stunning
her. And she would have thought that Krav didn't
have any more surprises in store for her. She understood that he was rich. It was just that she was also
beginning to understand that she didn't understand
what rich meant. In her tiny town in Georgia, she
had associated it with people with large flashy cars,
homes that were comically palatial, with all manner
of space that sat there unnecessary, simply creating
more volume as if it was entirely for the purpose of
shouting, *I could stuff all my extra cash in this space
if I wanted to.*

That was not rich. Not in the way Krav was.

There was wealth, she was beginning to realize,
that was not shouted about on the streets. Rather, it
was factual. A part of the way that he moved.

Every nook and cranny of the ornate estate that he
lived in spoke of this wealth. The way that he could
command the entirety of a boutique, yet did not call
attention to himself.

In fact, he seemed the sort of man who would be
happy to have no attention on him ever. But his bearing didn't allow it.

Everyone stared at him. Whatever room he was in,

whatever street he walked down, she had observed that people couldn't take their eyes off of him.

And neither could she.

The attraction between them...

He had not touched her. He had been solicitous to the point that she wondered if he still felt attraction for her.

But she felt it. Felt that slow burn inside of her, so utterly foreign.

She tried to imagine herself as the kind of sex kitten who would've gone back to his place minutes after meeting him.

It was difficult to do.

Almost impossible.

She had never wanted a man before him.

She did want him though. So that was consistent.

Even amidst all the confusion. All the...everything. She wanted him. She felt a deep curiosity about what it would be like to be touched by him. And an anger at the woman that she had been in that time before her accident, that woman who had kissed him. Touched him.

She was jealous of herself.

That thought made her laugh.

"What?" Krav asked.

"I just...nothing," she said, looking down. "It's silly."

She turned her focus to the beautifully appointed jet.

It had several rooms, and Soriya had been taken

back to the nursery by the nannies. She didn't love the involvement of the nannies, but Krav was very concerned about her sleep. Especially given all that her body had been through.

She appreciated it. But that was another thing she was jealous of. The world had had an entire month with Soriya that she hadn't. Krav had had that entire month. She...she had been sleeping. Sleeping through the birth of her child.

"I was actually just thinking that I am a bit jealous of myself," she said.

"In what sense?"

"It's almost like I'm the other woman," she said, feeling he touched her face. "I mean, because I've... I've been with you. But I don't remember. So it feels like...like it was an entirely different person. Not me."

"And you are jealous of yourself?"

His voice was practically a purr. Though, not the purr of a house cat.

"Well, you don't have to look like that."

"Like what?"

"So damned pleased with yourself."

"And how should I feel, knowing that my fiancée wants me?"

"Did you think that I didn't?"

He shifted, and his expression went to something like granite. "Things have changed between us, have they not? I take nothing for granted. As you said, it is... You are not a different woman, but it is as if we are living in a different timeline. Our past is erased. And so we must make what we can of today so that we might find tomorrow together."

"I don't think that will be difficult."

"I'm glad to hear it. Would you like a drink?"

She had not had alcohol since waking up. She was a moderate drinker anyway, but she had been very careful because of her mind and memory. She wasn't breast-feeding Soriya, because being in a coma the first month of a child's life, did make milk production problematic. Another thing that had been taken from her.

But she didn't want to focus on what had been taken from her. She wanted to focus on what she had been given.

This thing that felt like an utter surprise from the universe, all things considered. But she did feel the need to know what exactly had happened.

"What happened to me?"

"You were in an accident," he said.

"Was I by myself? Or were you in it with me?"

"You were alone. It is a regret of mine. You were driving early in the morning. You were hit head-on by a driver who had been out reveling all night."

"I must have been out very early," she said.

"Yes," he responded. "You were. It was… When I got the news of your accident… I have never felt out of control before, you must understand that. And yet you have challenged me at every turn. Challenged what I know about myself. And about my own power.

I would argue that it is good for me, except to have not enjoyed a single moment of it." There was a rawness to his admission that felt unfamiliar. That was ridiculous, since all of this felt familiar.

But this was different. She just knew that it was. "Then what?"

"You were taken to the hospital. And it was decided that you needed to deliver right away. It was quite precarious, that entire stretch of time. Not knowing if... If you or the baby would live."

"How awful for you," she said. "It would've been awful for me, but thankfully I remember none of it."

"You weren't conscious," he said. "You had a head injury upon impact."

"And so they gave me a C-section," she said.

"Yes. And Soriya was born. They monitored her closely, as she was early, but she was well. Healthy immediately. You... Your body protected her. Almost at the expense of itself. It was truly a miracle."

"Well, at least there was that."

"I brought you back to the estate. I did not wish to leave you to the care of the hospital. I hired my own staff to care for you, twenty-four hours a day. And a month after the accident, you woke up. But you did not remember any of the previous time we spent together."

"You've done so much for me. I'm sorry to have repaid you by forgetting you."

His gaze took on a distant look. "You're here now. That's what matters. In many ways, our relationship has progressed quite quickly. It is not as if we were a couple for many years."

"It's all very spontaneous, and I have to admit I tend to not be very spontaneous."

"No. Neither do I. And so it is a strange thing, I find. This union."

"You don't have any regrets, do you? Because you could get rid of me. You could've told me anything."

"I brought you here and kept you for a reason."

And she wanted him to say that it was because he loved her. Because she had assumed that he must.

But he had never said the word, she realized then.

But he must. He must. Because everything had moved so quickly.

You did get pregnant...

It made her wonder. If that was the only reason. But then, her mother had gotten pregnant, and it had meant nothing to her father. She didn't even know him. So it wasn't as if pregnancy meant by default that a man would marry you, stick by you, give you twenty-four-hour care in his palatial estate.

No. It didn't mean any of that. And so, she supposed she shouldn't worry so much about what words had been used or not.

And maybe, soon she would have the courage to ask. But until she could say it to him... She supposed she couldn't ask that he say it to her.

Though she was beginning to feel like... It was so strange. She couldn't remember even kissing the man, but she was beginning to feel like this was love.

Complete the survey below and return it today to receive up to 4 FREE BOOKS and FREE GIFTS guaranteed!

FREE BOOKS GIVEAWAY
Reader Survey

1

Do you prefer stories with happy endings?

◯ YES   ◯ NO

2

Do you share your favorite books with friends?

◯ YES   ◯ NO

3

Do you often choose to read instead of watching TV?

◯ YES   ◯ NO

YES! Please send me my Free Rewards, consisting of **2 Free Books from each series I select** and Free Mystery Gifts. I understand that I am under no obligation to buy anything, no purchase necessary see terms and conditions for details.

❏ Harlequin Desire® (225/326 HDL GRQJ)
❏ Harlequin Presents® Larger-Print (176/376 HDL GRQJ)
❏ **Try Both** (225/326 & 176/376 HDL GRQU)

FIRST NAME

LAST NAME

ADDRESS

APT.#

CITY

STATE/PROV.

ZIP/POSTAL CODE

EMAIL ❏ Please check this box if you would like to receive newsletters and promotional emails from Harlequin Enterprises ULC and its affiliates. You can unsubscribe anytime.

HD/HP-122-FBG22

She knew that she loved Soriya. It was instantaneous. The moment she had seen the child not only had she known that she was hers, she had been infused with an intense conviction that she would protect this child at all costs.

And that she would love her, at the expense of all else.

Because she did love her. With everything.

And so, maybe it wasn't so strange that she felt like she was falling in love with Krav.

Maybe it wasn't so strange at all.

And now he had answered her questions. About how it had happened.

She was glad she couldn't remember the accident, actually. How terrifying it must've been. But it was so hard to imagine what she would've felt in that situation, because she had no access to the girl that she'd been at that point.

So many things had changed in her life in the last ten months, and she couldn't remember any of them.

It was such a strange thing.

The plane touched down in Paris almost too quickly, and she would not have ever said that she would wish for a plane ride to go on longer, but the jet was just so lovely and comfortable, and her glass of champagne had warmed her.

She felt relaxed and…happy. That was the most amazing thing about all of this. She couldn't remember feeling quite so simply happy in all of her life. Maybe she was shallow. Maybe it had to do with all the money. And while she thought it might help, she really thought it was because of the addition of Krav and Soriya to her life.

"Does Jaia wonder where I am?"

"Jaia abandoned you, and I don't think she has worried much about you since," he said as they got into a limousine that was waiting for them at the airport.

"It's really no wonder that I'm so happy to accept my life here with you," she said. "Everyone in my life before was so…"

"Useless," he responded, the word carrying an edge, even as he grinned.

But that grin looked dangerous. And it felt like a knife-edge against her soul.

He knew her. Her flaws, her vulnerabilities. He remembered everything she'd ever told him. And he was…she felt things with a certain level of confidence where he was concerned, but it was nothing she could confirm. Nothing she could put into words.

She didn't *know* things about him. She only felt them. Whereas she was a book he'd read cover to cover and retained every word.

It felt exposing. Unfair.

"Well. Exactly."

"They are not worthy of you. I do not believe she ever inquired about your whereabouts. Though I think you did tell her that you had gone off to be with me. Likely, she's jealous. As I believe her greatest conquest during your trip was to shag a backpacker in a sad hostel."

She couldn't help it. She laughed. "That is so mean. But you know, Jaia probably enjoyed that."

"Indeed."

"I guess I shouldn't feel terribly proud of myself that when I decided to shag someone, he happened to be a billionaire."

He chuckled. "You didn't know," he said. And his eyes went molten. "You didn't know who I was."

"I didn't know you were rich?"

"No. The way that we met, it was not obvious."

"I'm… I like that."

She did. She loved the fact that she had simply met him and it had been right. This thing had bloomed between them.

They were whisked off to a penthouse apartment in the center of the city and what was practically a motorcade of their household help, and all of the baby items that they required.

The penthouse was yet another angle of beauty. Ultramodern, rising high above the classical architecture of Paris.

All glass and crisp clean angles high above lovely stone scrollwork.

It was unbelievable.

And she couldn't help herself, she twirled in the open space of the living area, with the Eiffel Tower behind her, and when she stopped, she was breathless, and he was right there. And she felt… Like it would be the most natural thing in the world to close the distance between them and kiss him.

And she knew she had done it before. Suddenly, she was overcome with the conviction that she had kissed that mouth hundreds of times.

There was heat in her belly that felt familiar, that same sort of certainty that clicked into place when she *knew* something about him that transcended a specific moment or memory.

But there on the heels of that heat was something…dark.

Something that held her back.

Suddenly there was a pain in her chest that felt so real she couldn't breathe past it, and it held her in place.

Kept her from touching her lips to his.

"What is it?"

"Nothing," she said. "I'm just… So excited to be here. With you."

She pushed the pain aside. She pushed the heat aside.

What she had, all she had with any certainty, was this moment.

She would choose to live in that.

They took a walk through the city. With Soriya in her pram, they saw the Eiffel Tower, the Champs-élysées, and they walked along the Seine. She was delighted and overwhelmed in the best way by all of the artists on the street selling their wares, and the bustle of the people around them. It wasn't only that she hadn't been to Paris, it was that she had been to very few major cities in all of her life. She was used to the pace of a small town.

And the speed and intensity of both Rome and Paris were a revelation.

After they were done with their walk, one of his beauty teams appeared, and ushered her into her suite, where she was given a facial, had her hair styled, and was wrapped in a haute couture gown—red and draped over her curves.

She looked in the mirror, and she didn't know herself.

Which should be something she was accustomed to by now, but she just wasn't.

The woman staring back at her was sophisticated. Her makeup expertly done, the bold red lip a choice she never would've made on her own.

But this was the woman that Krav loved. The one that he was going to marry.

Where is your ring...

And her heart fluttered, because she wondered... She wondered if tonight would be the night.

And as she looked in the mirror, she made her decision. Ring or not, tonight she was going to kiss him. Old memories, old feelings...they didn't matter.

She could sit in the unfairness of it all. That he knew more about her. That there were great swaths of their relationship she couldn't remember.

Or she could make new memories.

She wanted that. She wanted to follow that path.

She would start on it with a kiss, and see where it led. Because she was tired of being jealous of herself. Of a version of Riot that she couldn't access.

She had never once lived up to her name. At least… Not in her memory. So she would make a new one. Tonight. Where she was Riot, and that name meant something.

She was a bit nervous leaving Soriya, but she wanted to spend this time with him.

And she wondered if she would feel this tension no matter the circumstances. When she exited the bedroom, and went back to the living area, he was there.

And he took her breath away.

He was wearing a custom black suit that conformed to his lean muscled body. He looked taller, which she would've said was impossible, as she barely came to the top of his shoulder.

He was stunning. Arresting in all of his glory, but even now as he wore the trappings of civility with such ease, she sensed that wildness beneath. That tiger.

That danger.

And she wondered if she would always feel that as she stood there and looked at him. If she would always sense that underlying darkness.

And if she would ever know why.

If she would ever fully understand. "I hope you like dancing. I already know you like food."

"Yes. You do know me well."

But I don't know you.

That disquiet echoed inside of her, but she did not give voice to it. Because hadn't they spent all this time getting to know one another again? Hadn't he been kind and solicitous?

He had.

It didn't make that feeling go away.

But she ignored it.

She took his hand and let him lead her to the elevator, and then down to the street. There was a car waiting, this time not a limousine. This time a sports car, shiny and red, matching her dress.

They did not have a driver, rather he got behind the wheel, top down, and they drove through Paris as the streetlights began to illuminate. And she was grateful then that she didn't remember her car accident, because this was blissful, and she would hate for any notes of fear to sneak in and steal this from her.

Riding in a beautiful car with the most glorious man she had ever seen beside her.

The restaurant looked like a private residence, and the inside had much the same feel. Intimate and small, with very few tables.

"It is not the sort of place with a menu," he said.

She didn't know what that meant. But she was excited to find out. And find out she did, they were given a selection of the chef's favorites, the freshest foods that had been available today at the market, and turned into culinary masterpieces on the fly.

She felt drunk on food alone by the time they left the restaurant, walked down the street to another nondescript building which turned out to be what amounted to a speakeasy.

And for the first time since she had opened her eyes and seen him, he pulled her into his arms there on the dance floor. And her entire body was suffused with heat.

Held up against his strong body she…yes, she knew why she had gone back with him moments after meeting him. And the only reason they were waiting now was because of her amnesia, she knew that. He was concerned about her. And that was the only reason. Because otherwise they would have… This was undeniable. But suddenly she felt afraid.

She'd had a child since they'd last been together, and she had a scar on her stomach that hadn't been there before.

Maybe she wasn't as beautiful now. Maybe it hadn't been so much about her physical recovery, but about the fact that he didn't want her anymore.

"You're beautiful," he said, as if he could read her thoughts.

"Oh," she whispered.

"More now than ever. Riot, you are the most beautiful woman I've ever seen in my life, and it was true from the moment I saw you there at the ruins. And it is even more true now. All that you have withstood. All that you are. Beauty and strength. You have endured such cruelty from the world. And I will make it my mission to protect you from any more."

From the dance floor he led her up to the rooftop, where he got on one knee and opened up a box with a beautiful diamond ring, as fireworks went off over the city, illuminating the Eiffel Tower. As if he had made this moment just for them. Or perhaps he had. For when a billionaire proposed to you, she imagined there were very few limits on what was possible.

"Yes," she said. "I would marry you tonight."

And without rising from the ground, he grabbed hold of her waist and tugged her down to him, and on a growl, his lips crashed into hers. And she went up in flames.

CHAPTER SEVEN

SHE'D SAID YES. She was his. He would marry her as soon as possible, and she would be his. But first, he would brand her, with all of the passion that he felt in his veins. All of the desire that had been roaring in him like a beast all this time. All these months. Ever since he had first seen her.

It had never stopped. Monster, man, he did not see a difference between the two. And right now, he did not care. She'd said yes, and she would be his wife.

He held her face to his, as he kissed her deeper, his tongue sliding against hers, his need so intense he was not sure he possessed the fortitude to do anything other than strip her dress off now and have her on the rooftop.

He might've paid for a certain measure of privacy, but he felt as if that might be pushing it.

He consumed her, and she whimpered, arching her body against his, and he knew her. That was the unfair advantage, he supposed. He knew exactly what she liked, what she craved. He knew how to make her scream his name, how to make her beg for more. He had done it any number of times.

And yet for her this was the first.

That steadied him. Forced him to pull back, to soften the kiss, to turn it into a question rather than a command. Because for her this was the first time all over again.

He had taken her virginity once, and in many ways now he would do it again.

And what would he change? Now that he knew. Now that he knew he was the only man to ever touch her. Now that he knew he would have her forever.

His.

But had he not known that from the first moment?

The real mistake had been denying what was so apparently true. The real mistake he had made had been in believing Riot would not put him off his course.

Yes, that was the real mistake.

Now, he had corrected course. Now, he had made it so she would be his forever.

And when the years bled into years and they had been together longer than they'd been apart, the real story would be this one.

Not his mistakes.

Not his darkness.

They would both be with him.

She and Soriya, and everything would be as it should.

"Shall we go home?"

"Yes," she whispered. He cursed the fact that he had chosen to drive tonight as they waited for the car to be brought around to the front. He wished they were in a limo, so he could put the partition up and have her in the back seat. At the very least push her skirt up around her hips and bury his face between her thighs as they rode through traffic.

That would at least do something to satiate the desire that was growling inside of him.

Instead, he would have to content himself with knowing he would have her. Finally.

The drive took too long.

By the time they were back in the building, in the elevator, he could not wait a moment longer. When the doors closed, he pulled her into his arms, pushed her against the elevator wall and wrapped his hands around her wrists, forcing them up above her head as he kissed her neck, down to her shoulder, her collarbone.

"Krav!"

"Do you want me?" he asked, looking up at her, the intensity in him burning bright.

"Yes," she sobbed. "Please."

"Do you know what you're begging me for?"

She shook her head. "But I feel it."

"You want me to tell you. Because I know. I know just what you like."

And he did push his hand beneath her skirt, pressing his thumb against that sensitized bundle of nerves at the apex of her thighs and rubbing her slick flesh there. The first time he had touched her in all this time. He circled that sweet spot, and watched as her eyes went glassy. Watched as she began to surrender herself to this need. Her breath became short, choppy. And she began to roll her hips in time with the movement of his hand.

"You like that," he said. "You like it much better when I put my mouth there. When I lick you slowly, and taste every ounce of your desire for me. When I push a finger, and then another inside of you and mimic what we both really want. You like that a lot."

"Krav…"

"I'm not finished. You like me to do that until you're screaming. To eat you as if I am starving. And I am. With you I always am. You like to be teased." He took her hand, and guided it down to the front of his pants, moved her fingertips over his cloth covered erection. "You like for me to disrobe, and tease you with this. To toy with entering your body, but not quite. To deny you what you really want. Which is to be filled. You love that. You like to beg for it. And I like to make you beg."

Her eyes fluttered closed. "Look at me," he commanded, and she obeyed. "You're about to beg me now, aren't you?"

"I need… I need…"

"I know exactly what you want. And once we get inside the penthouse, I'm going to give you everything that I promised you here. And more. But you will beg for it."

"Yes," she said. Too soon, the elevator reached the penthouse. He had wanted to be in her instantaneously, but also wished to draw out this torture. She wasn't the only one who liked to be mad for it.

It was what they both liked. To push themselves. To make themselves wait for that moment of bliss. Sometimes they managed a mere thirty seconds. There had been a time in Cambodia when they had gone to dinner, and had made it into the entrance of the apartment, they had barely closed the door before he was inside of her. But they'd also had whole nights of teasing, tasting, denying themselves that ultimate release for as long as possible.

With her, it was always an adventure.

Tonight, though, he did not have the fortitude for games. Not long ones. Soriya was safely in bed, the entire place clear of visible staff, just as he had asked.

And he led her from the living room straight into his room.

"I want to see you," he said.

Her shoulders contracted in on themselves, and she suddenly looked shy.

"What?"

"I look different."

"You look beautiful."

And he took her in his arms and kissed her again, lowering the zipper on that dress as he did. Then he stepped back, and his desire became a living thing that he could no longer control.

Her curves were more generous than when they

had first met. And she had a scar, where their daughter had been brought into the world. All to him evidence of strength, of that time she could not remember.

Of that time that was lost to her, but buried in his memory forever.

That time they had been apart.

The time he had been sure he had broken her, but there she stood before him, not broken at all. In no way diminished, not even by him. And it was miraculous.

He unhooked the strapless, lace bra she had on and revealed her beautiful breasts to himself. Finally. His.

Her body was familiar, but this was like discovering her again.

"I know where I want you."

He took her hand and led her to the edge of the bed, then pulled her panties down as he sat her right on the edge of the mattress, spreading her thighs for him. He dropped to his knees. "I told you exactly what would happen," he said, looking up at her and reading her nerves accurately.

"Yes," she said.

"Will you beg for it?"

Her knees began to close. "I don't remember…"

"But I do. Trust me when I tell you, I have tasted you many times, and I am starving for you. I've been deprived of you for far too long."

Longer than she knew.

Ten months without this body. Ten months without sex at all, though he realized even if he'd had a hundred women since Riot had left his bed it wouldn't matter.

There had been none, but even if there had been, he would want her just as badly. Because sex on its own would never satisfy. Not again.

It had to be her. Only her.

"Please," she whispered.

And he took that plea.

He pressed his mouth against those slick folds, tasting that sweet nectar at the apex of her thighs. He sucked her, lost himself in her. In the sounds of pleasure that she made, in the way that she grabbed hold of his head and held herself against him.

She wanted him. She wanted this.

And he wanted nothing more than to drown in her.

He pushed his fingers inside of her, thrusting as he ate her, as her pleasure overtook them both.

"Please," she begged. "Please." He sucked hard, and he felt her explode, her orgasm almost everything he needed.

Almost.

"You," she said. And she began to work the buttons on his shirt, and he helped her, stripping himself naked, gratified by the rush of breath she let out.

"You're so beautiful," she said. "Oh… Krav."

And she leaned in, and kissed his chest, his abs, and he knew what she intended, but not tonight. He did not have the fortitude to withstand it. So instead, he lowered her down to the bed and pushed the head of his arousal through her folds, rolling his hips back and forth until she was sobbing. *"Please."*

"Please what?"

"In me," she said. "I need you inside me."

He grabbed hold of her hips and lifted them up off of the mattress, and he thrust home. Her cry of pleasure echoed in the room, and he began to move, losing himself in the rhythm of them.

The rhythm that only they had ever found together.

And he forgot. He forgot the game. He forgot what he was trying to do for her, because he could only feel. He could only feel this need. This desire. This everything. It overtook him, consumed him.

It was no longer about her first time.

It felt like his.

He thrust into her, grinding against her pleasure center, and she cried out, her orgasm rippling through her, and setting off his own. He growled, losing his control, thrusting into her one last time and spilling himself into her.

"Riot," he whispered.

And she held his head to her chest, stroking him as if he were a beast in need of taming.

But perhaps he was.

Perhaps he was.

"I love you," she whispered. "Krav, I love you."

He had done it. He had restored the things that had been lost between them. And she would be his.

His mouth curved into a grin as he pulled her into his arms and she rested her head on his chest.

He had won the war.

The war against himself, and all the darkness in his soul.

Riot was his. And there was no question about that.

CHAPTER EIGHT

WHEN SHE WOKE up it was raining.

Krav was still holding her in his arms, and she could hear his heart beating steadily against her ear. She could also hear the rain falling on the roof. Splattering against the windows.

It created the strangest echo inside of her.

For some reason, she felt compelled by it. There was a balcony off of the master bedroom, and she slipped out from the warmth of the covers, the warmth of his hold, and stood there for a moment. Looking at him.

None of his intensity eased in sleep. It was all still there. Except it seemed... Unvarnished.

There was nothing to soften it while he dreamed. His strength, the inherent danger of the man radiated off of him and sent a chill down her spine. And why should it?

He had been nothing but a romantic lover to her. Nothing but a man of extreme solicitousness. There was no reason to feel this chill.

She loved him.

She could see so clearly now how she had fallen for him.

The things that he had done to her body were magic. And no wonder she had given herself to him with such ease.

But it was more than that. He had given her the world. Quite literally. And for a girl from small-town Georgia, it was everything. It was like nothing she had ever even known to dream of. Private jets and Paris. Proposals beneath fireworks in the shadow of the Eiffel Tower.

How could she not love him?

She walked across the bedroom and stood in front of the glass door that led out to the balcony. She watched the rainfall, splattering against the surface. And then she opened the door.

She was naked, but for some reason she didn't feel self-conscious. She stepped out into that rain, and the drops began to roll over her skin. And there was a flash in her mind. Standing there at the root with him across the space from her.

Everything had changed in that moment. She knew it. She felt it. And most importantly, she saw it. Not because he had told her, but because she remembered. The rain. She had been soaked through to the bone, abandoned. Afraid. And he had been there. And she had wondered if she was walking to her doom or to her salvation, and she had chosen to walk toward him anyway. She always chose to walk toward him.

She hadn't known, even then. If he was a man or a monster.

Heated images flashed into her mind. That night in the tree house. It had been a tree house. She had given herself to him without thought. Because there had been no room for thought. His hands on her body. His mouth on her throat. Would he use his teeth to destroy her or give her pleasure? He had given her pleasure.

And she knew now why it had all seemed so strange. Because she had unlearned so much about life that night. And built something new. New affirmations inside of herself that changed the very foundation of who she was.

It amazed her, that realization that so much of the changes had taken place over the course of a single night. But they had. Utterly. Absolutely.

And the rain continued to pour down her skin, and as the drops washed away the fog in her mind, she could see further and further into time.

They had not separated after that night. Not ever. She had been in his bed every night after that. She felt like she was running through an open field, racing toward something in the distance.

Sun and truth, even as she stood still in that cleansing rain.

Rain.

Rain again. She was running through the rain.

On the streets, cobbled and uneven. And she fell. But what happened before? What had happened before that moment? She could remember holding her stomach. Low. Blood.

And as clearly as if she was experiencing it now, she remembered looking up, raindrops hitting her face. Melding with the tears on her cheeks.

I'm losing it anyway. Everything is lost.

And it was his face she saw. But there was none of the gentle lover there. It was the Tiger. Only and ever. Dark and fearful in his symmetry. And there was no terror over whether he would devour her, for he already had.

In that moment, everything had been gone. Everything she had believed about herself, all of the new truths that he had built that first night, decimated. The future. Everything she had hoped for. Everything she had believed in him. But most of all, he was gone. The man that she had grown to love was gone, all of his artifice ripped away, revealing the truth of him. That deep, horrific darkness that she had sensed was beneath the surface all that time.

But she couldn't connect the whole memory. Only that picture. Only that face.

And the blood.

She stumbled back inside, soaking wet and shivering, and Krav sat up in bed, threw the covers to the side, revealing his glorious, sculpted body.

But she felt nothing more than wild, insensible terror. "What did you do?"

"Riot…"

"No. I need to know. I remembered the rain. I remember the rain and the day that we met. I remembered why I went back with you. I remembered… You changed me. You made me feel like I was beautiful. But then it rained again, and you made me feel like I was nothing. You destroyed me. You destroyed us, didn't you?"

"Riot…"

"No," she said, moving away from him. "You never loved me. You don't love me." He had never said it. He had never said it, but she had believed that he did because he had to. Because how could they be here building this beautiful life together with their beautiful child if he didn't love her?

"You never loved me. And you… You sent me away. You did."

She couldn't remember, but she could feel it now. She could feel the utter brokenness in her soul. As if her heart had been severed from her. That was that moment. He had done worse to her than anyone else in her life ever had. Because he had made her believe that there could be more. He had made her believe that he cared. And she had been a fool. She had ignored all of the things that her spirit had known. Had sensed. She had chosen to see only his beauty, and to ignore his darkness. She had chosen to believe that just because he could make her feel good didn't mean he would eventually destroy her with that danger.

She had mistaken the fact that a predator could be beautiful for a promise that he would be *good*.

But he was still a predator. And he would destroy that which stood in his way. Krav was a man who consumed beautiful things, sated himself on them until they no longer served him.

She knew it. In that moment she knew it.

He was not a beautiful man with the touch of predator. He was the Tiger.

All the way through.

Anything else was simply a facade. A gleam of gold and stripes to distract, of burning eyes, dancing fire that hypnotized and left his prey stunned, immobilized, willingly standing there waiting for the strike. And strike he had.

She had wanted so badly to remember… She had wanted so badly to remember.

The falling in love. But it didn't exist. Oh, she had fallen in love with him. And he had slaked his lust with her.

He had *used* her.

Nothing more. She had told him everything about herself, and she couldn't remember him because he had told her nothing. Nothing. The only truths she had ever learned about him were during that first night. That first night when he had told her about his mother. But it had been nothing more than basic facts. Nothing more than the barest hint of information. There had been no real emotion behind it. She had put it all there.

Because she had wanted to see it.

She had created a beautiful life for herself, and he had been there, the scaffolding for it.

But this…

He had lied to her. He knew that she didn't remember, and he had lied.

"Tell me," she said, her throat tightening. "Tell me the truth."

"We should be together," he said, his voice scraped raw.

"Why? Why should we be together?"

"For Soriya," he said. "She needs you."

"I can take care of her fine on my own."

And that statement jogged more of her memory. It was the after. She had left. She had left him after that night in the rain, after the bleeding and the pain.

And suddenly, grief spread out through her chest like a poison.

She had lost him. And for a while she believed she had lost her pregnancy. But she had gone to the doctor when her period didn't resume a few weeks later, and they had confirmed the viability of her pregnancy. The bleeding didn't mean she had miscarried.

But she had spent the pregnancy alone. And Krav hadn't known.

"What happened to me?" she asked, her heart pounding so hard it made her dizzy. She was sick with it, with this.

Staring down the man who had become the ultimate villain in her life. And she'd fallen in love with him a second time. It made her wish for that blankness again. It made her wish she knew nothing, because knowing this truth about him, about herself, was too much to bear.

She'd fallen for this man a second time. Even though somewhere inside herself she had to have known what he was.

"I told you the truth," he said. "You were in an accident. It was how I discovered you were still pregnant."

"Oh. Because you thought that I had lost the baby. And you… You sent me away anyway."

His expression hardened. "You left."

But she could see herself, curled up in a massive bed in his empty house. Then could see the staff carefully taking her to the car…

So gentle, all that betrayal. Wrapped in soft sheets and sent away in a limousine.

But it was rejection, a mortal wounding all the same.

"Because you wanted me to. You might not have thrown me out into the street, but you made it clear you wanted me gone, and if I hadn't left you probably would never have returned to the villa. Don't rewrite it even now that I remember. But you're right. Then I wanted to. I never wanted to see you again. Ever. You destroyed me. You took my dreams after you gave them to me, and there is nothing crueler than that, Krav. And you knew that if I remembered…

You know if I remembered I would never want to see you again."

If only she could remember what had led up to that moment outside. If only she could remember. But it was like her brain had the door firmly shut on it. Like it didn't want to know.

"I made a new life for myself. Away from you. Away from your rejection. Why did you get to hold her first?" The question came deep from her soul. "Why? Why should you have memories of her birth when I don't? You didn't want her."

And that statement threw the door open on all the memories. "I told you I loved you," she said. "I wanted to make a life with you. I believed that we could."

The devastation was raw and real. That dinner. The way that she had hoped and believed. That he had loved her the way that she loved him. And this was just the same. He had lulled her right back into that fantasy. And this time… Oh, this time it had been even more cruel. Because he had made her believe… He had made her believe. Again. What a fool she was. And he was happy to make her one.

He moved toward her, and she jerked back. "Don't touch me. How dare you. You made love to me with me thinking you… With me thinking I loved you. When we both know I don't. Not anymore. Not ever. I want to go. I'm leaving. I'm taking Soriya back to England."

"I'm afraid that is not possible," he said, his face shadowed in darkness. "You are to stay with me."

"I don't want to."

"And how do you think that will go for you, Riot? I am one of the richest men in the world. You have just sustained a head injury. I have been caring for Soriya all this time... And I cared for you."

"You rejected her."

"You ran away and nearly caused yourself to miscarry. I did not chase you out into that storm."

His words were hard and harsh, and she knew they were a lie. She knew he didn't even believe this version, and yet she could see him trying to hold it up over himself as a shield now.

This was the Krav she'd forgotten.

The man who used his cruelty to guard any tender places in himself. To push anyone who got too close far, far away.

"Is that what you tell yourself? Your cruelty wasn't the beast that ran me right out of your villa? I did not miscarry. I went on to make a life, I got a job, I had a home..."

"You have a home with me. You will still be my wife."

"This changes everything."

"It changes *nothing*."

His words landed, a cruel blade at the center of her chest. "It changes nothing to you if I go from loving you to despising you? It changes nothing if you go from having a wife who stays with you willingly to one who is a prisoner?"

And again, she saw the truth of him. He lifted a shoulder and shrugged. Worse, he stood there naked, as if it bothered him not at all, while she felt increasingly vulnerable, soft and exposed.

How could you go up against a man such as him?

A man who felt nothing.

"I want to leave," she said.

He took a step toward her, his eyes all black fire. "I don't care."

"You would keep her from me?"

"Yes. Because in the end, you won't go. Not if I keep her. And so, I will have what I want."

"Why did you do this? Why do you care? You've never…" And it was like a light had been shone into all the dark places in this glorious life, this glorious home. No more illusion left at all. "I've never even seen you hold her."

He had made sure she was cared for, but he never touched their daughter.

He never showed love.

And her mind, her heart, her soul, had been so desperate to fashion him into what she'd wanted him to be that she hadn't seen it, not really.

The blind spots hadn't come solely from her lack of memory.

She wanted love so very badly.

His love.

She'd wanted his lie to be true, so she'd ignored anything that had shown it for what it was.

"She is a Valenti," he said. "She will have my name, my protection, and all of my power behind her. And she will have her mother. You had literature on adoption in your car…"

"I was given pamphlets by a doctor, and didn't clean out my purse. You don't know anything about me, Krav, you don't want to. You listen to my story, and yet you heard nothing. You don't know who I am. You don't care to know."

"What matters is that you are her mother. She needs her mother."

The words were rough and wild. How could he seem to feel nothing and everything all at once? She couldn't understand this man, and she'd believed once that she did.

Because she could turn him on? Because they'd shared sex and passion?

It was such an innocent thing to believe.

She'd had all his intensity focused on her in the bedroom and she'd believed it had given her the key to knowing him.

But it was a darkness that ran deep, and she couldn't see the bottom of it. A terrifying void that drove him, that haunted him.

He seemed cold and unfeeling, and yet it was more.

He burned.

But the flames were black.

"And the jailer?" she asked. "Standing in place of a father?"

"It isn't like that."

"Isn't it?"

"I will protect her. I will protect you." The promise was guttural, honest. Of all the things he'd said, she knew this was honest.

But he was missing the truth of it.

He had the power to hurt them both. More than any other person on earth.

"From everything but yourself?"

"I did not ask for this."

"Oh, you didn't ask to be a father? You just had sex with me without a condom."

He growled. "I did not ask for this thing between us."

This thing.

This passion.

It tortured him, she could see it. He didn't lie. And it hurt her. To know that the most beautiful thing she'd ever felt had been anathema to him all this time.

"What a victim desiring me has made you," she spat. "I cannot imagine how difficult it is." He took another step toward her, and her traitorous body responded. To the beautifully sculpted lines of his nude form. Everything in her wanted to launch herself at him. Scratch his face, and then kiss him. Hurt him, and then make love to him.

She shuddered. In repulsion. But not at him, at

herself. At what he had made her. For he had changed her, at her very core. Her very foundation, and she had believed it had been for the best, but it had not been.

He had turned her into his creature, and she hated that girl.

At least the woman she had been, scarred though she was by her mother, without friendships, or attachments, had been independent. What was she now? "I hate you," she said. "As much as I ever thought I loved you. You have killed us. It will never be the same again."

"It was never love for me."

He burned in this flame, but it didn't consume him. And it threatened to make her ash. It was too hot for her. Too devastating.

"I won't marry you," she whispered.

"I believe you will."

The threat in those words did not escape her. He would take Soriya from her if he had to.

"I want my own room."

"By all means," he said, his voice hard. "Keep this one."

He did not bother to dress, he simply strode from the room, closing the door tightly behind him, and leaving her. She collapsed to the ground, and there was nothing. Nothing but the sound of the rain and her own piteous weeping.

Riot Phillips had thought for a moment that she was loved.

And what a cruel trick it had been.

She had all her memories now, she had the truth.

And she wished desperately that she could go back to living a lie.

Because it had been such a beautiful lie.

You can't live a lie.

You can't.

So this was the truth. All sharp and jagged edges. But what did it gain her?

There was no dignity to be had here. No respect.

She was utterly reduced.

You will remake yourself. You have every time.

And this time you have Soriya.

And that right there was the bright, burning conviction she needed.

A fire that would burn hotter than that demonic flame in Krav.

She was a mother. And she could remember now. That pregnancy. And how it had gotten her through the heartbreak of losing Krav.

It had sustained her. Soriya had sustained her.

She put on a robe, and walked out of the room, moving slowly to evaluate whether or not Krav was still in the main part of the penthouse.

She crept into Soriya's room. She looked down at her tiny, sleeping daughter. "I will not be my mother. And whatever happened to your father... I will do better. I will not allow you to become twisted and bitter. Or sad and lonely. You will be better for having me. I will not be weak. And I will not lose you.

I will do whatever it takes to protect you. I promise." And she realized then it was Soriya who was protecting Riot. For she was giving her purpose. She was giving her strength now. Something bigger than simply her own heartbreak.

Because she was broken. She could be as angry as possible, holding that up as a shield to herself but as much as she despised him now, she had loved him.

And that was terribly painful.

But she was resolved.

She would do whatever she needed to do to be with Soriya. It was her hill. She would die on it.

And given that she was living with a tiger, that was very, very likely.

CHAPTER NINE

HE HAD BEEN caught in his own trap. He had spun a web so very deceptive, that even he had begun to believe it. Had begun to erase the truth of what had happened between them the night she had told him of her pregnancy.

Had begun to believe in the connection that they had created.

But it was a lie. A very clever one, but a lie nonetheless.

And now... Now she hated him.

She had not lied. She had spoken with the full force of truth.

I love you.

I hate you.

He had heard both things from her last night, and both had been true.

But it did not change his resolve.

He knew what he had to do.

But...

She would never let him touch her again.

There was a strange echo in his soul that reminded him of when his mother had died.

It felt like grief. He always felt as if he was standing some distance away from his emotions. Examining them from afar, looking at them with some dispassionate distance.

And so, this was not a crippling feeling, rather it was simply there.

She was right. He had never held Soriya.

Because he had that distance. And it was a valuable thing. It served him well.

It mattered.

He had been torn from his mother's arms when he was five years old. He had not seen her again until he was an adult, who could make his own decisions and do what he wished with his time.

He had found her. The reunion had not been what he had hoped.

She had been so broken, bent by all the years of sorrow and poverty. Of a hard world and emotional devastation.

She hadn't liked to look at him. In his suits. She hadn't liked to hear him speak.

Still, she had mattered to him.

But it had been too late for him.

When he had been ripped away from her, it was as if he had been torn from his own heart.

The intensity of it had been too much for his small body to bear, and he was convinced it had damaged his ability to connect after. That and the general cruelty of his father. It had provided him with protection, and he did not regret it. But she made him wish...

She made him wish things could be different. That he could be different.

He'd had moments of it. When he'd been trying to change this story for the both of them. He'd had moments where he'd found gentleness in himself he hadn't known was there.

But that wasn't real. It had been an act.

It had to have been.

Nothing good in him could survive, or thrive or last.

The next morning, she was adamant that they leave.

She was like ice as she looked at him.

"I just want to go back to the villa. Where there is...*space*."

Unspoken he thought that was also...where he had not touched her.

"You're through with Paris?"

"I have a feeling I will be through with Paris for the rest of my life. I don't know that I should ever like to return here."

"That is a shame. Paris has quite a lot to recommend it."

"Paris can go to hell."

He had never seen her bitter.

After their... Their breakup, he supposed, all those months ago, he had not seen her again. She had been sad then, but he had not been on the receiving end of her anger.

But now he was. And it was quite stunning in its force.

"We will marry next week," he said.

"How nice for us," she said.

Their plane ride back to Italy was astonishingly different than the ride over. She did not look around the plane and delight. She did not flirt with him.

She sat, ashen, and she held Soriya the entire time. Like a tiny shield.

And he had not realized… He had not realized all the warmth that she injected into his life. Until she had taken it from him.

She had only been awake for a couple of weeks, but even while she had been in a coma, he had been able to imagine what they might build.

You bought into your own lies. More fool you.

It didn't matter. He was accomplishing his end. She wouldn't leave now. Wouldn't leave Soriya. She would marry him.

And someday… If there was one thing he knew it was that the desire between them would overcome this anger.

She would not withhold her body from him forever.

That made him feel better.

He knew that she wouldn't, because it was inevitable.

Because they were inevitable.

Whatever she might think.

"Why are you like this?" she asked, with only twenty minutes before they began their descent.

"Why am I like what?"

"I have racked my brain, Krav. And one thing I do know. You never shared yourself with me. The night of your mother's funeral is the closest that I got to knowing anything about you. But I don't even know... I don't know your story. Your parents. How did they meet? I don't know who raised you I don't know..."

"I didn't know my mother," he said, deciding now to simply tell it. It did not have to touch him to explain the truth of it all. "Not really. My father was on vacation in Cambodia, he had an affair. With a beautiful woman who worked at a bar he went to. He was much older than she. He had no children. And he needed them. Some years later, he discovered that she had given birth. To a boy. He wanted me. Not because he cared about anyone or anything but himself. He took me from her, and left in my place a sum of money. But she had no choice. She had no choice. I was taken away from everything I had ever known. My home. My language. My mother. Taken to Italy and raised by a man who inflicted nothing but pain upon me. You're right, I have not held Soriya. I'd rather never touch her than do to her what my father did to me. I can protect her without... Without being him."

"What makes you think you would be like him?"

"It is a chance I would rather not take. When you spent your life raised by a monster, it is bound to seep into your blood."

"Krav... He took you from your mother?"

"Yes. I had spare little time with her before her death."

"But you kept a home in Cambodia..."

"Yes, my father always had a hotel there, it was why he was there in the first place all those years ago. I went to visit my mother as soon as I became an adult and began to form an uneasy... I don't know. We would see one another sometimes. Eventually I decided to have a personal residence there to...to reconnect. With the food, the language. My people. I was raised Italian. That will always be the biggest part of me, and there is no going back and rewriting that. It was the place I spent most of my life. But Cambodia was my foundation. And... I felt an impulse to try and go back to that."

"It's as much a part of you as Italy."

"I suppose. Though, not in practice."

And now he had told her. Dispassionately, the truth of things.

And she seemed... She seemed as if she didn't know how to react.

"You never told me any of this."

"I don't speak of it."

"You nearly did. That first night we met."

"I was not myself. I was not here."

And obviously he did not mean on the plane. He

meant in his father's world. In his father's world, there were rules. And they had to be followed. Otherwise, there were grave consequences.

And yes, it had been different. In his homeland, the land of his mother, grieving her loss.

"What did your father do to you?" She asked. The pressure in the cabin began to change. "We have begun our descent," he said. "There is no time to get into what my father did to me. But suffice it to say, whatever monster you think I am, you're not wrong. I was made to be this way. I was made to be able to run the Valenti empire with no weaknesses standing in my way. No attachments. He succeeded in making me into his…his creation. Perfectly cold and capable of doing whatever needed to be done. I'm sorry that you were brought into this."

It was the truth. The most honest thing he'd ever said. It felt…freeing to admit it.

"Are you?"

"Yes," he said.

"Then you can't be entirely without feeling."

"My feelings are ghosts. I might know they're there, but I can't grab hold of them. And the minute I try…they vanish."

The plane landed then, and they got in a car that carried them back to the estate.

"We will live separate lives," she said, when they got back to the estate. As they stood in the vast entryway. And suddenly, he remembered standing there as a boy. And how large and imposing everything had been. How large and imposing his father had been.

"As long as that life is contained here."

"Why do you feel the need to control it if you don't care?"

"It is...it's the only thing I know."

And he didn't know what that meant. Only that it was true. And it echoed inside of him long after the words were spoken.

But as time marched on, as their wedding drew nearer, that persistent feeling of grief wouldn't go away.

And he remembered...

He remembered when she had not. When she had believed he loved her.

It had been easy in its own way. All he had to do was take her to nice places, speak to her with kindness. All that he had to do was pretend the past didn't exist.

It had felt...

It had been a strange sort of freedom. The first time he'd felt detached from what his father had made him.

He didn't see why they couldn't do it now. He didn't see why.

And what he wanted was to find his way back to that, he realized.

It stunned him. The realization that he wanted something. The realization that he missed...her. Of course, when she had gone the first time he had missed the sex. That had been what he told himself. But they'd only been together once. In all this time, only once.

And it was not simply that he missed.

He missed her, and he missed the child being around. She was around less when Riot wasn't there. Of course. It made sense.

He had been filled with certainty. That nothing mattered but the wedding. Joining her to him. But he was beginning to realize it wasn't enough.

To live in this space. Of darkness. Of utter coldness between them.

No.

And on the eve of the wedding, he made a decision. He was going to win her back. With her full memory, he would win her back.

He could not fix what was broken in himself. But she felt like the key to something.

When she'd loved him, he'd been in control of his darkness in a more profound way than ever. He wanted that back.

He would make it so.

She would love him again.

Of that he was certain.

CHAPTER TEN

SHE WAS DOING her best to be as happy as possible. But she had lost that feeling of being the luckiest girl in the world. It had been there for a while. And it had been so intoxicating. The feeling of having it all.

She had Soriya. She lived in a beautiful place.

She might be desperately lonely, but that was not really any different from the life she had before she had known Krav.

And at least she had a child.

That was an unexpected gift, and something she hadn't thought she wanted.

To be a mother.

But there was healing taking place inside of her soul as she mothered her child.

As she was able to find space to heal over the ways her mother had not been there for her.

She was able to consciously consider how to be there for her own daughter.

She was able to put that intention into words and plant them deep inside of her own heart as she held her, saying to her as they lay out on the grass in the estate.

And sometimes she would look up and see Krav, gazing down from the balcony over them.

And she did her best not to look back.

Did her best not to think about him at all.

But it was hard.

She had said that she hated him as much as she had ever loved him, and that was true. It was just that… Sometimes she felt like the hatred existed right alongside the love.

Especially after what he had told her about his past. About his father. His mother.

He had said it with such detachment. It was difficult to understand exactly what he felt about it.

But she had been turning it over inside of herself. Deciding what she felt about it.

And it was an incredibly difficult thing to parse. So mostly, she chose not to.

But she was marrying him. She was marrying him. That was… Such a strange thing.

She had also been grappling with all of her memories. That was the problem. She had gotten that broken, bad memory back. The truth of what happened when she found out she was pregnant. And she felt utterly silly for having romanticized it now. But she had also gotten back the time they'd had together. And there had been joy in it. And she had seen a lightness in him, and she didn't think it was a lie.

It was only that… Finding out he was going to be

a father had terrified him. She could see that now. That of course he would react to fear with anger. And she could understand that there was fear because of his own past. His own childhood. It made her soften. Which irritated her.

But there was so much more to him than he thought. Than was easy to see.

He'd said he was cold. That his feelings were ghosts, but she'd seen how untrue that was.

His rage was not a ghost. It was a whole dragon.

And if he felt that with such intensity, he must be able to feel everything else.

It was all buried, twisted and mangled beneath the rubble left behind by his childhood. And that made her feel…

She didn't want to find any sympathy for him. Not any softness. That way lay a certain measure of madness. Because she just wasn't…immune to him. As much as she wanted to be. And the man was forcing her into marriage…

You could leave. You could fight him.

She pushed that thought away. She wasn't particularly interested in thinking about the ways in which she was responsible for the situation she found herself in.

It was easy to think only of the way that he had stormed into her life. Easy to think of herself as a lamb being led to slaughter.

She thought of that even as she was wrapped in

her white wedding gown the day of the ceremony. Yes, a sacrificial lamb. That's what she was.

Spotless on the altar before him.

So much drama.

But Riot embraced the drama, as the bouquet of red roses was handed to her.

And she wondered who this farce of a wedding was for. If the doors would swing open and the church would be full of people who were strangers to her.

But the Cathedral was empty. Empty of everyone except for him. The nannies that held Soriya acting as witnesses.

He was alone. And that stood out as stark as the fact that she was too.

And right then, as she walked down the aisle toward him, with no one forcing her or marching her in that direction, she suddenly saw all of those missing memories again. But she saw them differently.

She had walked toward him in the ruin. She had gone with him back to the tree house. When he had pounced, when he had kissed her, she had returned it. With just as much force and greed as he displayed.

And that made everything feel different.

Did a lamb return volley when the Tiger pounced?

No. And she knew it.

Only a tigress did that.

Only a tigress would ever stand against something quite so fearsome.

And she saw in that moment every responsibility that belonged to her.

She had wanted him, and she had had him. She hadn't asked him to use protection. She hadn't cared.

She had wanted him, and so she had taken him. She had wanted to leave her life behind, and she had allowed him to do that, she had allowed him to not share with her because she hadn't wanted her fantasy disrupted.

And when he had sent her away, she'd been heartbroken, because she had allowed herself to see him with rose-colored glasses, and she had done it not out of innocence, and not out of a misunderstanding over the way that the world worked, but rather because she knew quite a bit too much about how people were. The abandonment of her own mother, of her father. She hadn't wanted to lose him, and she hadn't wanted to know that he might not be as wonderful as she had first thought him to be. No, she hadn't thought him wonderful at first, she'd thought him dangerous.

She had just wanted him to be the fantasy, so she had willfully set out to make him into one, and she had broken her own heart. He had never made her a promise. Not ever.

She had hoped, because she was still optimistic despite whatever life had thrown at her. And she wondered if…

She wondered if what she had really wanted all

this time was to have adventures but to be able to blame other people when they went wrong.

She might've been bitter at Jaia for the lack of planning on the trip, but she hadn't contributed any planning to it. She had paid her own money and gone sailing off after her friend. Knowing that she was flaky.

And then she had gone off with Krav, with no more planning about where she would end up.

And so, every pitfall was someone else's fault, wasn't it?

But no. They were her choices. It was her heartbreak. She had chosen it.

Just as now she was choosing to walk down the aisle toward him while she told herself she hated him. And yes, he had put her in a difficult situation. He had put her in one with options she didn't like.

But that was not the same as being forced. Even now, she was walking down the aisle toward him because part of her hoped.

Because whatever she said, whatever she told herself, she had not lost hope. Not entirely.

About what they can have. About who he could be. But she had to stop being passive. She had to stop fantasizing. And she had to be honest. She could not see herself merely as a victim. She had to see herself as an active participant in all of this.

And if she wanted more from him she had to demand it.

No. She had never done that. Instead, she had

fallen desperately in love with him, with a facade, because she had allowed herself to fashion him into the image of something that she wanted him to be.

So maybe she needed to set about learning more about him. And see if she could fall in love with that man. The one that she had professed to hate.

He had hurt her. And yes, when she had woken up, she hadn't remembered that he had done that. So what she had learned from that experience was that she would fall for him again every single time. Because there was something in him that was undeniably for her, no matter what. She could call it chemistry or sexual desire, and surely there was an element of that involved. But it also couldn't be quite that simple. It couldn't be quite that limited.

She thought of all that and realized her own power as she was walking down the aisle toward him.

It stunned her.

And as she stood before him, as he took her hand and brought her to that place in front of the priest, she was faced with the enormity of what she was doing.

She was making vows to him. Becoming his wife. And that was not a temporary state. If she was going to stand there and promise him forever, then perhaps she needed to be prepared to fight for it.

At least give it a try.

A real try, an honest try.

Grappling with the man that he was, and not simply the one she wanted him to be.

Maybe he could change.

Maybe for Soriya it was worth the endeavor.

And maybe for you?

She had not touched him since that night, and now they held hands and faced each other.

"Do you promise to love, honor and obey one another, as long as you both shall live?"

"I will," he said.

And then the question was posed to her. What did that mean? Had he even paused to consider it? Or was it merely part of his plan to keep her with him? She looked into his dark eyes, and she wished that she could fully understand what it was that he wanted from this. He wanted Soriya to have a mother, but was that all?

What she was realizing about herself, just now, was that there were issues handed to her in childhood that she was aware of, but that did not mean she fully understood the ways that they impacted her life.

And she could see some of them as she looked back on her interactions with Krav.

It was just not as simple as she would like it to be.

And so when she said, "I will," she did so knowing that she didn't truly understand what she was saying. Or what it would mean for them. What it would look like. She did so knowing that they had a long road ahead of them, and that she could not let him have the final say in this marriage.

On what it would be.

And when it was time for them to kiss, she made a decision. To go into that kiss. To go into him.

Their mouths met, and her heart nearly burst through her chest. This thing between them had always been so glorious, so wonderful. This was the easy part. This desire. Except it cut her now. Made her feel a deep sense of desire, loss and pain. And of hope. And it was the hope that hurt her most of all. That thing with wings, but she worried that if she flew too high, that in the end, it might abandon her. That it might be part of her destruction.

They were pronounced, man and wife, and they joined hands and walked down the aisle, to their audience of two, and when they had exited the sanctuary, she looked at him.

"Have no fear," he said. "I have no designs on claiming a wedding night. You are free to spend the rest of the day as you wish. You are my wife, you can go spend my money abroad if you wish."

"I think I would like to go home. And take care of our daughter."

"Then you are free to do that if you wish as well."

"Does cruelty make you feel better?"

He paused. "Are you attempting to score points?"

"No," she said. "I am simply asking you a question. Does cruelty make you feel better in this instance? Does it make things seem clear to you? Because I understand that we do things in an attempt to make them seem simple. I personally liked to rewrite what I wanted into fate and fairy tales. Because it meant I didn't have to be responsible for the decisions. So does being cruel absolving you from needing to be better?"

"You think I'm being cruel, but I am just being that which I was made."

He believed that. She could see it. But she felt in that moment that she knew differently. That she could see the way that he was working to simplify all of this for himself. To justify.

And she didn't know why he needed it. She just recognized the same thing that she witnessed in her own self. And he left her there, but there was another car to take her back to the estate. They did not go together. He did not seem concerned in the least about appearances of any kind.

Their relationship had already been in the media, and they'd made no announcements about their wedding, so they had drawn no attention for the event.

She wondered if it would've been different, had she not remembered.

You know it would've been. You would've worn that dress in front of a sanctuary full of people.

Yes. She would have. He would've given her the wedding of her dreams. He would have been the solicitous groom. And he would've taken her to a beautiful hotel, where he would've laid her down on silken sheets after and given her a glorious wedding night.

And she wished, in that moment that she could have the fantasy back.

It would've been so much easier.

It was this damn reality. That was what made things so difficult. And she wasn't angry at herself for seeking the mists of fantasy. She knew why she did it. It was just she couldn't do it. Not now. Not with everything she knew. Not with everything she was. Everything she had become.

She ate dinner alone.

She spent the evening holding Soriya, rocking her. Reminding herself that this was why she was doing what she was doing.

No. Because at some point you need to be doing something for yourself.

That realization cracked her open.

She saw her mother as selfish, so she had determined that she would simply become the best mother to Soriya that she could possibly be.

She had thought that her own desire shouldn't come into it. That it couldn't come into it. And she realized with absolute clarity that was just as potentially damaging as being a selfish mother.

She had to know who she was. She had to be able to show her daughter what life could be.

She couldn't see herself as a lamb. Because she wasn't one. She was a tigress. Wasn't she? She was too. She had survived everything that she had been raised with. She had done it well. It wasn't that she didn't have issues. But she was acknowledging them. She had survived. She would give Soriya better. And she would make sure that she knew from the beginning that she was a daughter of a tigress, and that she would be no less. That she was brilliant and wonderful, and that she deserved the whole world.

But she would have to demand things for herself. Otherwise...

Those lessons would be empty. If she saw Riot meekly accepting this sham of a marriage, a life without love, if she saw her wandering around like she was a woman in chains, then how would a message of empowerment mean anything?

And anyway, it was just more hiding. To go from a fantasy straight to martyrdom. To decide that she hated him when nothing inside of her was anything near that clear or simple when it came to her feelings for Krav.

No. It was more. It was everything, just as he was.

Everything ugly and complex, but the good things remained.

And that was when she made her decision.

She kissed Soriya on the forehead and laid her down in her crib, and then she went down the hall. She was dressed in nothing remarkable. It was not a wedding night ensemble.

They made love in Paris, but she hadn't remembered the truth of them. She did now. She remembered the way that he had hurt her. But she also remembered the foundation of their connection. The heat between them, so undeniable. The way that she had always craved more, even if they had just finished making love. The way he had transformed her, from someone who was afraid of this sort of desire, to a woman who had embraced it.

The memories were complicated. And so were they.

And so was she.

In her sweats.

Without knocking, she opened the door to Krav's bedroom.

He was standing in front of his nightstand, shirtless, wearing the dark pants that he had worn in the wedding, and nothing more. His feet were bare, and just as it had seemed that first night they were together, there was something so intimate about that.

She wished that they could go back there. To Cambodia. She remembered vividly seeing him in the clothing native to his country—the silk sarong in a rich blue, flowing over him like water, rather than the rigid, fitted suits he wore away from there—and how…right it looked. How fitting.

This life was one that had been forced upon him. In the same way he was trying to force it onto her. But perhaps he knew no other way. And perhaps he didn't think anyone would choose this life, this life with him, if there wasn't force involved. What else had he been shown?

He had shared with her, and she had tried her best not to feel sympathy.

He had not shared it seeking sympathy. He had not shared it with emotion, but that didn't mean it wasn't there.

It didn't mean it wasn't there.

"What is it you want?" He asked, straightening, setting his watch down on the nightstand.

She looked at his chest, broad and covered in dark hair. She was hungry for him.

Emotional turmoil aside.

But she wasn't here simply because of the hunger. Simply because she was driven by desire for him.

No. She was here to try and make a new map of them. To draw them back to each other, so that they might be able to meet somewhere.

She did not wish to live in this house with them living different lives. Moving on different paths. She wanted to find a way to join him.

She was hurt. She was still terribly hurt by him. And this wasn't going to make it go away. Not entirely. This wasn't even really forgiveness. It was just reclaiming. And she needed that. She needed it desperately.

"I want my wedding night."

She stripped her sweatshirt up over her head, and she had nothing underneath it.

And in spite of the fact that nothing she was wearing was particularly sexy, she could see him respond.

The fire in his eyes was instant. Burning bright.

"Why?"

"I don't know," she said. "But it's my choice." She pushed her pants down her hips, and took her underwear along with them. She had been naked in front of Krav any number of times. Countless times, and she had all of the memories now. She had been shame-less with him. And she would be shameless now.

"But you didn't force me into this marriage, I chose it. I'm choosing to be here now. Because what I want matters. I don't want a cold marriage. I don't want to simply be married to you and wander the corridors pale and listless, behaving as if I am one of your victims. I'm not a victim. Anymore than you have victimized me. I made choices that brought me here. I made a choice to be here now."

"But, do you want me?"

"Yes. You know that I do. That has never stopped."

"But, you do hate me," he said, his eyes lit with black flame.

"Yes," she said. "Part of me does. Part of me will never understand why you treated me so cruelly. I loved you so much, Krav. And you destroyed that. You looked at me as if I was nothing. As if you hated me."

"I never hated you," he said. "Only myself."

The words hit her like a blow. He said them as if they were a simple statement of fact. Something that cost him nothing. And yet…she felt it. Deep and echoing in her soul.

"And what do you feel for me?"

"I don't know," he said. "Because I lost the ability to truly feel my emotions the day I was taken away from my mother. And I'm not saying that to garner sympathy. You have asked an honest question, and you stood there and gave me honesty, so I'm trying to do the same. It doesn't cost me anything to admit it. I'm broken."

"Why? Because he said you were?"

"No. Because he was. And he raised me to be. And it doesn't matter if I know, maybe in ways that he never knew such a thing about himself, the fact remains the same. I have learned to stand back and look at my feelings, but I have not learned to actually experience them."

"I don't believe that. I believe that there's more."

"Don't. Don't go down that road with me. I don't actually want to hurt you."

"You're willing to. Emotionally."

He nodded slowly. "Yes. I am."

"Perhaps I'm willing to hurt us both. I told myself when I met you that you were a predator. And I felt nervous. As if I were prey. But I never behaved like prey, did I? And I won't behave like it now."

"Riot," he said, his voice rough. "I want to possess you. And that is the truth of it. I have from the moment I saw you."

"I want to possess you," she said. "You were the most beautiful man I had ever seen."

"But you can't."

"Can't I?"

She moved toward him, and pressed her body against him, and she could feel the evidence of his desire for her pushing against the front of his slacks. "You want me, and you cannot help yourself. Was there another woman? In all the time I was away from you?"

She would accept the answer, whatever it was, but the idea of him touching another woman made her see red.

"No," he said. "I have not been with another woman since the first time I laid eyes on you."

"So I have you already, don't I? You came for me. Even though you said you didn't want a child. You came for me. What made you change your mind?"

"I didn't want her," he said, his voice jagged. "I simply knew... I thought that you didn't want her."

It angered her to hear him say that. She knew it was...she knew where it came from. That it triggered deep pain from his childhood. But it still wounded her. "You know now that I do, and you still married me. You still want to keep us. You want to keep us together, you just want to keep us at arm's length..."

"It isn't that I want to, it's simply that it's how it is. It's how I feel."

"You lie. But not most especially to me. Most especially to yourself. You lie to us both."

"Are you here to screw me, or are you here to talk?"

"We can do that if you'd like," she said. "That's what we did. A lot of it. Though...sometimes I was making love."

"I never was. I never am."

He was pushing her away. She could see that. He never knew what he wanted, and she could see that too. He wanted her close and the minute it was too much, he broke.

She didn't want to allow it, not now.

"And that's why you care so much for my pleasure."

"Why don't you stop talking," he said. "And see to mine."

A surge of power filled her, and she recognized her choice in this. That she wanted to do this. That she wanted to use his desire for her against him.

Her feelings were not simple. Because her anger at him was still there.

It was just there was more than that. And for all that he said he couldn't feel his emotions, she felt them all.

She was overwhelmed by them. Rage, desire, need, and love. Still love.

She hadn't ever wanted this. Something so messy. She had her fill of difficult people. And yet somehow this was different. Because he wasn't detached from her.

Her mother would go in and out of her life on a whim. Her friends had done the same. But he couldn't. He'd married her. Whatever he said, he had married her. He had taken steps to keep her with him forever, and that was different. He was different. And so… She was willing to take this on.

She wanted to.

She sank to her knees in front of him, working

the belt on his pants, opening them, revealing that glorious, hard length of him.

She had always thought him beautiful.

She loved his naked body.

She had always liked the look of men, but she had never been tempted enough by them to do anything.

He was a constant temptation.

She leaned in, sliding her tongue over his length, the way that he had taught her to pleasure him.

She took him deep into her mouth, sucked him until he was groaning with desire. Until she had the power. All of it. And she knew it well.

Until she couldn't wait any longer. Until she needed him between her thighs, not just her lips.

She stood then, pressing against the center of his chest, and he sat on the edge of the bed. She straddled his lap, bringing herself down onto his hardened length and impaling herself on the evidence of his desire.

She let her head fall back as greed overtook them both. He gripped her hips, and brought her down hard onto him every time she moved, increasing the intensity even while she set the pace.

And they didn't kiss. It was more primal than that. And there was too much… It was still too much anger.

But he was hers. And he was in her. And she needed him. Needed this, in ways that she couldn't articulate.

"Krav," she said, rolling her hips forward.

"Riot."

And he came inside of her on a roar, and she followed him over the edge, need pulsing through her, memories.

She made love to him knowing that they had met in a rainstorm. Knowing that they carried on a torrid, physical only affair that spanned continents. Knowing that he had rejected her. That he had sent her away thinking she had lost the baby. Knowing that he had lied to her. That he had manipulated her.

And wanting him anyway. Having him anyway.

And when it was done, their foreheads pressed together, their breathing jagged.

"I don't know what our marriage will be," she said. "But it will not be in name only."

"Be careful," he said, tracing a line down her throat with the tip of his tongue before kissing her. "You may not be happy that you've opened up this possibility."

"Whatever we are, how can we find out if we build fences around each other?"

"I live my whole life with the wall between myself and the world, Riot, and marriage will not change that. Sex will not change it."

"Maybe it isn't for you. Maybe it's because it's changing me."

"As long as I get to have you. Doesn't matter."

She wished that it did. She wanted to tell him that it should. But instead, she simply slid away from him and collected her clothes. "I assume you won't stop me from keeping my own room?"

"Is it what you want?"

She wanted to protect herself, and she understood that was the urge driving her now. But for now, she was going to give in to it.

"Yes."

"All right."

He was still naked, still breathing hard. And yet speaking with such cool dispassionate emotion that it would be easy to believe he hadn't been affected. If she hadn't just had him inside of her. If she didn't know better.

And when she went back to her room, she gave in to her own complicated feelings, and started to weep.

Because she might've resolved to take action, and to be strong, but that didn't mean it was pain free.

No, this thing was difficult. This thing was a fight.

But at least now she had admitted that.

She was his wife, but not by command, by choice.

And that meant the marriage would be something of her choosing.

CHAPTER ELEVEN

SHE HAD NOT come to his bed again since the wedding night. It had been three days, and it was all he had thought about.

She had been a revelation, had Riot.

He had been restrained, allowing her a measure of control when what he wanted was to pull her to him and keep her with him all night.

But there was something reckless in her emotion, as if he could see her balancing on a knife's edge, willing to risk anything, and... He was not a man who admitted to fear, but he was a man who knew better than to push a woman when it was ill advised.

As if you have ever been in a similar situation with another woman.

No. Never. But then there was no woman other than Riot.

He was left unsettled by the entire experience, and he would like to say he was not a man who did unsettled, anymore than he was one who did uncertainty or fear, but he felt as if he had done a host of things he didn't normally do since Riot had come into his life.

And it was difficult, because he didn't do entanglements, and yet just like they had done at that simpler time, they shared meals together at night. And it was unavoidable that they talk.

And she knew things about him, about his past and the way that it made him feel, and now, about the things he did every day.

Because she had begun to ask. And he did not deny her answers to the questions.

About his life. His mother. His business.

She was different than she had been before.

He had not been forthcoming with information about his life, and she hadn't pressed. But she pressed now.

And he could feel her winding herself more tightly into the fabric of who he was.

And she would do all this while holding the baby.

He felt protective over the child, but...

He had still not held her.

And soon enough, she would be bigger. And you did not hold larger children anyway.

He could not remember being held.

And one night, he was walking down the halls, and he heard plaintive wailing. Usually, Riot wasn't far behind when the baby was upset, or the nannies. But nobody came.

He pushed open the door, and walked into the

room, it was shrouded in darkness, and so was the tiny bundle.

He stood there. And watched her cry. He stood there and watched her cry because…

He had convinced himself that somehow his touch would be more damaging than his distance.

The child was crying, and he was doing nothing.

He had been this lonely child. Denied a hug, and comfort, and the arms of a parent. And here he was, doing the same.

He was a coward.

He would've said that he was not a coward, he would've said that he wasn't afraid, but he was a man steeped in fear, and he could recognize that then. He was not disconnected from it. It took him over. It made him feel choked with it. Not with the fear, but with disgust for himself.

He took a step closer to the crib, and closer still.

Then he reached down, and touched that tiny, flailing hand. And she stopped. And curled her fingers around his.

This tiny girl holding on to him with everything she had. And he remembered. Clinging to his mother. And he had convinced himself because of that memory that a child needed a mother. Because he had been devastated by the loss of his own, brought to a world where he had a father, but that father had meant nothing, that father might as well not have been there.

But he had needed both. And he hadn't had them.

Not really. The tragedy was not that he had been taken from his mother and raised by a father, but that no one had raised him as a parent truly should.

And that was the crime. And here he was, perpetuating pain of a different kind. Passing it on to this child who was innocent, who didn't deserve this.

Who needed him to find it in himself to be more. To be better.

It was because of Riot that he was standing here even now.

Because of who she was. Because of her bravery. Because of the way she had treated him these past days, even when he didn't deserve it. Because of the connections she was trying to build.

His chest felt heavy with it. With the realization of it all.

And in that moment, he realized that no matter his intent, he was going to keep that cycle spinning. Unless he did something. Unless he changed.

He leaned down and, using the same technique he had seen the nannies and Riot use, supporting her head, he lifted her out of the crib and cradled her to his chest.

And the strangest sensation overtook him, and it wasn't simply possessiveness. It wasn't simply a desire to protect. It was that, but it was more. The absolute conviction that he would not just die for this child, but he would live for her as well.

That he would do everything he could to ensure that she didn't experience the pain that he had in his life. But she wouldn't experience the pain Riot had either.

And this was why, he knew. This was why he had never held her before. It was because he had known that if he did this, he would have to change.

And he had decided who he was a long time ago. It was protection. To throw up all the walls that he could as quickly as possible around himself and en-sure that nothing and no one could reach him.

He had cemented himself in his earliest days, a defense against his father. Not allowing him to de-cide who Krav was going to be. Not allowing him-self to be movable.

He had done it to consolidate the core of who his mother had made him. To save a piece of himself from that assimilation. To keep his heritage. To keep his happiest days.

And so, change had been his enemy.

But he had to do it now. And it wasn't about force.

No. His father had used an iron fist to try and ef-fect an evolution in Krav.

Instead, it was the delicate, tiny fist of his daugh-ter, wrapped around his finger that had changed him.

It had been the kiss of a woman at the ruin. That had begun this journey. This moment. This change.

It was like a blow to him. He could barely breathe past it.

He stood, and cradled her, swaying back and forth as he did so. And then he looked up, and he saw

Riot. Standing there in the doorway. With tears on her cheeks.

"She's asleep now," he murmured, laying her back down in the crib.

"I didn't know she was crying," Riot said.

"It's all right." His chest felt tight, and he didn't want to speak of the things he had just recognized. He didn't know why. He didn't know why it was so difficult. To stand in front of her with all of this rolling through him and try to make sense of it. Try to find words for it.

Instead, he moved away from the crib and walked toward her.

Put his hand on her face, and leaned in to kiss her. They hadn't touched since their wedding night, when their coming together had been intense and wild.

But when he kissed her this time, it was softer.

He broke away from her, pain lancing his chest, and he turned and walked away, out onto the expansive balcony that ran from the nursery along the side of the estate. It overlooked that place where she usually lay out with Soriya. Where he usually stood over them and watched, but didn't partake, because he held himself back.

And it was raining.

He looked back at her, and she stepped out onto the terrace with him.

"Why is it always raining?" he asked.

When he met her.

When she left him.

When she'd remembered.

"Maybe it's trying to tell us something," she said.

And she walked toward him, the sky truly broken open now, beginning to go from light to downpour.

But she didn't flinch.

Instead, she put her hand on his face. "Maybe it's trying to grow something new. That's what rain does. It creates new life."

He swept her up into his arms, lifting her up off of the balcony, and kissed her.

Kissed her without end, as the water washed them both clean. He carried her down those stairs of the balcony, to the place that he had watched her, but not joined her before. The place that he had held himself back from.

So much holding himself back.

She stripped his clothes from him, he from her.

And they were naked, down on the blanket that she kept there, raindrops sliding down their skin, as his hands skimmed over her body.

She was beautiful and wild, delicate and strong all at once.

She was everything in a way no one else ever had been.

And she had been from the beginning.

Krav was a person who had spent his life in isolation.

He had held onto a dream about where he was from. About his mother. But they were disconnected. He had visited her often, but they had never felt like mother and son. And in the end she was so ill he wasn't even certain she knew it was him who was there.

And he had attended that funeral in that same isolation. Sitting in the front with everyone around him giving him a wide berth, because even if they were family in a distant sense, they didn't know him.

He had been robbed of that. Not just his mother, but a community.

He had been brought to Italy where he hadn't been given one. And yes, he had wild success.

Money. People flocked around him because of that. Because he had power.

Women wanted him because they thought he was handsome, but most of all because they thought he could give them something.

There were a great many men who didn't look like him, who had any number of feminine acolytes because they could write a check and make the world's problems seem that much smaller.

None of what he had, none of what he'd built had anything to do with him.

But Riot had been there. She had been with him. She had seen him.

And they had made something together that night. Just as they were making something now.

It was more than desire. Connection.

Tiny, tenuous golden threads, woven around them and through them.

Shoring up the broken places inside of them. Knitting them back together. Leaving veins of gold dust where before there had been darkness.

Emptiness.

Nothing.

And when he sank into her beautiful body, he was electrified. Lit up from the inside out.

But that light shone on the darkest of things, and they didn't scurry away. They were there. Staring back at him. There was nowhere to hide.

And it made him want to retreat.

But he couldn't. Because she was all around him. Soft and smelling like sunshine and rain. Like revelations.

His release was something more than pleasure. It emptied him out. And what remained...

What remained...

He rolled over onto his back, the rain cascading down his chest as he lay there, eyes open in the torrential storm.

And she covered him. Put her body over his and curled up against him, her hand over his chest. They were together. And he remembered, when she had been on the ground before him with all that rain.

He remembered, the way that he had treated her. Even while his heart raged against him. Those feelings...

Those feelings he tried so hard not to connect with.

Is it just the way it is, or is it something you've made?

He sat up. "We should go inside," he said. "You will be cold."

"Will I be?"

"I'm afraid you will be, yes."

"I'm never cold when I'm with you."

But there was something in her eyes that made him think she was lying.

"I don't think you mean that," he said.

"I would like to mean it," she said. "From now on. I would like to mean it."

He knew that she had felt cold with him. Because he had turned her away. And in turn, he had turned away from her.

But no, he wanted... He wanted her love. He wanted her love.

And he recognized that he was going to have to... be different. Do different things. But surely there was a way to keep what needed to be kept secure, kept secure. Surely there was a way...

"Ask for whatever you want," he said. "And I will give it to you. Even if it's half of my wealth."

"I don't want your wealth," she said. "I mean, I'm quite happy to live in it. But I just want us."

He picked her up again, naked this time, and took her into the house wet. He brought her into the shower, and let it warm them both.

Then he carried her to bed.

And he made love to her again in the softness of the sheets. And he thought... This was more than he had ever sought to build for himself.

He had been given back a piece of something.

He may never have a whole heart.

But perhaps she could be that heart.

When he did things that pleased her, then he would know. He would know that it was right. That he was right.

He would know.

And he slept with that knowledge, with that comfort.

He might be broken beyond repair. But there were places she had put him back together, and where he could not be… She could be his compass.

He held her. All night long.

And for the first time in memory, he dreamed of the future.

And he did not despise what he saw.

CHAPTER TWELVE

THAT NIGHT WITH Krav had been transformative.
Whatever had happened between them… Whatever
had happened in him. He had held her.

And he had kept on doing it in the days since.

They had begun to share a bed every night.

But it was different than the time they had spent
together on the Amalfi Coast. Different than that
reckless, sexual affair.

Not that what was between them wasn't deeply
sexual, it was.

But there was something else to it. He truly let
her make love to him.

But he…

He was still holding himself back. Of that she was
certain. He was still… Fighting something. Fighting
the two of them.

It was a subtle thing, but she felt it. That there was
a resistance inside of him that didn't want to crum-
ble. And yet… He had softened.

It wasn't that she didn't still look at him and see

a predator. She did. Because he was. Every bit as dangerous as he had always been. But something in him had changed.

Still, she didn't quite… She didn't quite know where they were at.

And she didn't quite know how to approach him. He had hurt her. Many times. And if there was anything she had learned in life it was how to protect herself. She had been foolish with him on multiple occasions. Had held her beating heart out to him only to have him reject it. Or worse, crush it beneath his boot heel.

She didn't want to do that again. For obvious reasons.

A fool's errand, as it was.

And then he suggested they go to the Amalfi Coast.

And she had no idea if she was ready to visit the site of her previous degradation. But she agreed. Because… She felt compelled to follow this path they were on.

She felt like there might be answers there.

It was a joy to watch him take part in packing Soriya up for the trip. Watching him participate in fatherhood, rather than simply presiding over it as a man who was being forced to bear witness to it.

He was the one who packed her diaper bag. And bundled her up, ready for the trip. And on the plane, he was the one who held her.

"I've never held a baby before her," he said when they were comfortably in the sky.

"Never?"

"No. I was… I was very isolated in my life."

"Can you tell me more about your childhood?"

"Will you be charging hourly for the session?"

"No. But I just… I want to know. One of the things that I promised myself was that I would be a good mother to her. No matter what happened between us. My childhood was lonely," she said. "We moved a lot. We had to, because we were dodging landlords. Creditors. Always. So I might make friends at school, but it would be for a small moment. And sometimes my mother didn't even enroll me in school because we weren't in a place long enough. It was very fractured, and it was extremely uncertain."

"Tell me," he said. "What were you planning on doing? Really. You didn't tell me that you were still pregnant. You must've had a plan."

"I didn't tell you because you said you didn't want a child."

His jaw firmed and he nodded slowly. "I did. I'm not angry at you for that."

And yet there was anger in his voice. But she wondered if it was mostly directed at himself.

"Well good, if you were angry at me for that, I would have to punch you in the stomach, because you don't deserve to be angry at me for what I did to survive."

"No."

And somehow, that resonated inside of her. What she had done to survive. She looked at him, and she wondered how much of what he'd done was trying to make sure he survived.

It created sympathy where she hadn't expected to feel it.

And she wanted to continue to press him about his childhood, not allow him to derail the discussion with her own stories. But maybe he needed her stories.

"I knew I wanted to give her stability," she said. "And most of all love. Support. I was an afterthought to my mother. She dragged me along with her, and I think she often resented it. I made her life harder. I was very aware of that. I wanted… The reason that I was a virgin, Krav, is that I never wanted that life. I thought that I was smarter than her. And I met you, and I threw it all out the window. Because smart… There was no being smart. I just wanted you. And I threw everything I knew out the window for that. But when I found out that I was going to have Soriya… Well, then I knew I had to be better. I got a job in England. I decided that I would stay there. I didn't want to go back to Georgia because I didn't want to feel like I was living the same life my mother was. And maybe that was just a feeling, and something I did to make myself feel… Better. But I got a job, and it was a good one. I found a decent living situation. I was delivering baked goods when I got into my accident."

"Do you remember the accident?"

"No. I still don't. The last thing I remember is going in to work. I don't know that I'll ever remember the accident. It scares me, a little bit. That lost time. But I gained some of it back, so… Anyway, I did have a plan. But I think the most important thing wasn't the plan. It was recognizing where my mother failed. And promising in my heart that I wasn't going to let her decide my path. I want to decide it."

"You are strong," he said. "I'm grateful my daughter has such a strong mother."

"Tell me," she said. "What was it like growing up in that state?"

"It was a nightmare," he said. "Mostly, my father only had oversight with me via tutors and nannies. They were told to be hands off with me. Not coddle me. But sometimes… He was a violent man, Riot. And sometimes there was a fury in him that could only be expressed on me. But even that… I found ways to survive it.

"The worst part was knowing I'd had something different. And losing my connection to that day by day. Bit by bit. Until love wasn't even a memory, it was simply a picture in my mind, an impression of a feeling rather than the feeling itself.

"And as I moved further and further away from that… I moved further and further away from everything. It was how I survived. That distance."

"Krav…"

"They aren't pretty stories."

"No. But life isn't always pretty. And I want to know you. You can tell me. You don't have to simply make broad sweeping statements about all the things that happened. You can tell me exactly what it was."

"He once beat me so badly I thought I would die. So did my nanny. She took me to the hospital, but they had to hush up what had happened." He stared off into the distance, his eyes dark. "And I remember it. Every blow. Every kick. Over and over again. And if you cannot escape physically, you go somewhere inside of yourself. I don't know if I ever made it back out."

Survival. Everything he was, was because of what he'd done to survive.

And it broke her. Destroyed her. That this man had been through so much. That he had been so badly treated. "I survived despite him," he said. "And when his health failed, I removed him from this house, I sent him away. I put him in a facility, and I never saw him again. There were no bedside declarations. No deathbed rants. I let him die alone. And I hope... I hope that in that moment, when hell opened up to greet him, he was as scared as I was when I was a child. As alone. As cut off from everything he cared about. His money didn't cushion him. Not in the end. And the only reason I even put him in a medical facility was so that he could live in such a reduced state." He looked at her. "Do you think me cruel?"

"Yes," she said, answering honestly. "But I don't blame you for it."

"It is interesting, isn't it. I tried very hard not to let him decide who I was. But the thing that I feel the most... The thing that I feel the most connected to is that rage that he left for me. And the cruelty. Sometimes that concerns me."

"It doesn't concern me."

"Have you ever wanted revenge on your mother?"

"No. She's too sad. She never had any power. She never had any power, so she rebelled continuously against the world around her. Against her own choices. Revenge would accomplish nothing, she was an eternal victim, and it would simply give her more things to justify herself."

"You are kinder than I am."

"I don't think I am. I'm not sure what I would've done if the opportunity presented itself."

They looked at each other, and she felt... Burdened. By all these things between them.

But she cared for him. Deeply.

And she felt less... Justified in being upset about returning to the home on the Amalfi Coast. Because he lived in the place where he had nearly been beaten to death, and he managed to deal with it. She recognized now that whatever Krav had done, it hadn't been out of cruelty.

He was just trying to survive.

He had made a bad choice in a bid for that survival. A hurtful one.

But everything between them was fraud, and they were not going to make it through all of this without hurting each other. They would probably do it again.

It was just… It was just how things were.

There was something in the acceptance of that that made her feel calm. She couldn't explain it.

They landed at the villa, and her heart went tight.

Yes, she really had been hurt badly here.

But now there was a nursery.

And it was beautiful.

It reminded her of the bedroom that he had done for her at the estate. The bedroom she didn't sleep in anymore, because she slept with him.

"This is beautiful."

"It was important to me to have this place for her."

"You've changed," she said to him, putting her hand on his face.

"Have I?" And there was a thread of desperation behind those words, and they broke her.

"Yes," she said.

It was strange to walk around this place, this place she hadn't been for nearly a year. And where she had been… New and hopeful in her connection with him, but not deep either.

They hadn't known each other. She couldn't get him to share things about himself.

And now it was different. They were different. But there were barriers still.

And she wondered if they had the strength to get through them.

Don't lose hope.

And she had no idea where that voice came from. Because there was nothing in her life to suggest that hope meant anything.

Liar.

You're stuck thinking about your childhood. Not this life with him. There is every reason to believe that hope means something.

Hadn't they endured so much already? And they weren't apart from each other, in spite of all the things that had happened. They were still together. They were married. Krav was her husband and that had to count for something. He had told her about his childhood. About the trauma that he had endured. The abuse.

That mattered.

They had both had so many chances to walk away. And even if they had done for a while, it hadn't stayed that way.

There was hope in that.

There was hope.

And it was here that she'd said she loved him for the first time. And she'd said it again in Paris.

And each and every time something in her had been broken after.

Each and every time.

She wondered if she had the bravery to say it again. Because she did love him. She did. She had from the beginning, and learning about him had only deepened it. And now she had scars, scars from him.

She liked to think he had a few from her.

It hadn't been easy to get here.

But they had a marriage, and they had a child. And he was no longer holding himself back from Soriya. So that had to matter.

And maybe she was too attached to echoes. To rain. But she decided to plan a nice dinner for the two of them. Like that night everything had fallen apart. Because she was determined to write them a different ending. Because he was her fate. She had known it then, and she knew it just as deeply now, so perhaps what was required was trusting in that. Trusting in them.

She had the same dinner prepared, maybe she was a glutton for punishment of one kind or another. She wouldn't be surprised. She wouldn't be surprised if there were things and issues in herself she didn't fully comprehend. But here she was.

The nannies had Soriya taken care of. Tonight was about her and Krav. It was important. And necessary. Tonight was about the two of them.

Their connection, but also everything they had learned since that night. That night they'd met.

She had believed their connection had been chemistry.

But it was more. Deeper. And it grew deeper every day.

When he came downstairs from his day working in his office, he was dressed in a white shirt, two buttons undone at his strong throat, the sleeves pushed up to his elbows, revealing strong forearms.

He was beautiful, and she would never tire of him. Of all that tanned, toned skin. His perfectly chiseled features. His large, strong hands and the way that they held her.

"I thought tonight was special."

"Why exactly?" he asked, looking down the table.

"I thought it was special because we were together."

"We are always together," he said, kissing her on the lips.

"I know," she said. "That makes life feel kinda special."

He pulled away from her slowly, a cautious grin on his face. "I suppose."

"I'm not going to tell you I'm pregnant."

He laughed. "That is a relief."

"Do you want more children?"

He paused for a moment. "I'm not opposed. You and I are both only children. Perhaps Soriya should have siblings."

"I think I'd like that," she said.

And maybe that was the point of the dinner. To plan for the future. It made her feel light and happy. It made her feel hopeful.

They ate in relative silence, making occasional companionable conversation.

This felt like the real connection she never had with anyone in her life.

Deep and special.

But… But something was missing. Something was missing.

She swallowed hard, committing to making it through dessert at least.

She didn't know where the disquiet inside of her was coming from.

And maybe the problem was she was being like a ferret, feeling the need to weasel at something endlessly.

But it was this one thing.

This one thing.

When they finished dessert, he held out his hand, and she stood, responding to his call. He pulled her down onto his lap, kissed her, and she could taste dark chocolate and coffee, mingled with desire.

"Krav," she whispered. And she had every intent of telling him that she loved him. She wasn't afraid to tell him. She had told him so many times.

But she stood there realizing that… They had done it before. And they needed to stop repeating things. Here she was in the middle of an echo of a night many months ago. How many echoes had there been?

But something had to change.

Something had to change.

"Do you love me?"

CHAPTER THIRTEEN

HE HAD NOT expected that. He had been awash in victory.

He had won her back.

It had become abundantly clear over these weeks. She was no longer withholding herself from him. She was happy to be with him, just as she had been in the beginning. He had her. He had her in that way that he craved. In the way he had never had another person. Not in his real true memory. She cared for him. And it had felt like victory. He was confident he had gotten to a place where she no longer hated him. That place they'd been in that dark, hideous night.

When the worst parts of him had been on display.

And she had said one of the words he had expected. But she had flipped it. And it had sent everything in him to a grinding halt.

And he found that he... That he couldn't respond. So he wrapped his hand around her head, gripped the back of it, and pulled her down to him, kissing her hard and fierce, because it made sense. Because it… Because it let him move further away from that question.

Because how many times could they do this? How many times could she pull away from him? How many times…

How many times could he run?

This isn't running. And words don't matter.

He kissed her. With all of the pent-up ferocity inside of him. And this wasn't that time out in the rain. It wasn't sweet or tender. It was fearsome. Because everything in him was. A tiger threatening to devour them both. But him most of all.

An ache inside of him blossomed, grew.

Made it all untenable.

He didn't want to feel this. Didn't want to want.

"Krav…"

"Don't speak," he said, nipping at her jawline. And he could see that tears filled her eyes as he continued to kiss her, but she didn't push him away. She didn't pull away.

And he growled, biting her on the side of her neck, and kissing down further, wrenching the straps of her dress down and exposing her breasts to his gaze.

His staff would know better than to interrupt. They knew how it was between the two of them.

Inevitable.

Dark.

Is that because of you?

He had thought the sun had gotten in. And it had. For bright moments it did.

But then there were these walls. These things. That she asked for, that life asked for, that he couldn't respond to.

That he couldn't...

He couldn't. It was impossible.

It was impossible.

And so he kissed her, because that he could do. He lowered his head and sucked her nipple into his mouth, because he knew that. Desire. He knew need. And he knew how to slake the lust that sparked between them. But he did not know how to answer this question.

He didn't know. And he wasn't a man who trafficked in uncertainty or fear, and here he was made of it. Because of her.

Always because of her. Because she had come into his life and she had demanded things of him that he didn't know how to answer. Because he had brought her here, to this very place, at this very table, this very moment, and she had told him he was going to be a father when he couldn't even think of the word father without everything inside of him turning to stone.

And he had found a way around that. He had. He held the child now. He... He cared for her. And he cared for Riot too, why must she continually demand more?

Why does it not end?

It was a foolish question, because it wasn't simply coming from her. The desire in him wouldn't end either. It didn't stop. It didn't change. There was no way to staunch the flow. The flow of this need.

It was endless. And he could not control it.

And that was what he found unacceptable. Unendurable.

Her hands went to his chest, tugging at the buttons on his shirt, and he could feel her rage. It was nothing less than rage.

She was angry about all of this. About wanting him. About the way he was responding to her question. Then yet still, she couldn't keep her hands off of him.

He made the mistake of looking into her eyes. And he could see there, a kind of desperation. A request that reached down into his heart and tugged.

And he could not find the distance that had carried him through life up until this point. Even that moment in the nursery with Soriya paled in comparison to what one simple look from Riot did to him.

He felt like his guts had been torn out. Like his heart had been grabbed and squeezed. Crushed. In the delicate palm of her hand. And only she had the power to do this. Only she could destroy him like that. And it was utter destruction.

He could not look at her. He couldn't.

He lifted her up off of his lap and pushed her up against the bar. Pressing her hands flat to the marble top. He swept her hair to the side and kissed the back of her neck and she shivered.

And he waited. To see if she would tell him to

leave her. To see if she would push him away. But she didn't.

He pushed her dress up past her hips, pulling aside the silk of her underwear and pushing his fingers through her slick folds.

She was wet for him. Even now.

Just as he was hard for her. No matter that the world was burning around them.

No. There were no flames. They were all inside of him. He was a light. Tortured by this devastation raging inside of him. Tormented by her. All that she was.

He had seen her as a gift that day. Waiting at the ruins for him. Waiting to satisfy his urges, something that he could bury his grief in.

And yet, she had not helped him bury his feelings at all. Ever since he had first met Riot all she had done was call deeper feelings up to the surface. She had not been a gift. She had been a curse. This long road of attempting to recover from the death of his mother...

These things could not just go on hurting.

The world could not keep delivering endless pain. What was the purpose of it? What was the purpose of any of it? He growled, pushing two fingers inside of her and wrapping his fist around her hair, pulling it back. She arched her spine, pressing her bottom more firmly into him. Letting his fingers go deeper.

"You want me even now," he said. "I cannot give you what you want, and yet you desire this."

"You won't give me what I want," she said, looking over her shoulder, her eyes glinting.

"You don't understand," he said, working his fingers in and out of her. "I can't."

"You're a coward," she said.

He growled, freeing himself from his pants and thrusting into her in one smooth stroke.

He gripped her hips hard with one hand, held her hair with the other, and he punished them both. For needing each other like they did. For all the feelings that this created inside of them. If he could open his chest and pull his heart out, take out everything that offended him, he would.

But he could not. So here they were. Lost in this maelstrom of need.

And when his desire overtook him completely, he roared out his release, as he felt her break apart, tremble and cry out as her internal muscles pulsed around him.

"You may not love me anymore," he growled, "but you need me."

"I didn't say I didn't love you," she said.

He moved away from her.

"But you don't."

"I do. I really, really wanted to make you say it, Krav. I did. Because I have torn myself open for you time and time again. Only to have you tell me no. Only to have you look at me and tell me you don't feel things the way that I do. But I can see now that… I have to. I have to, don't I? Nobody loved me either.

You don't have a monopoly on pain. On parents who are distant. Who don't care. The difference between you and me is that I want to love. I want to. I want to be loved. When I woke up from that coma, and I thought that we were in love, it was like every dream I had never even known I had had come true. And maybe that's it. I had that moment. That clarity. It was all that mattered. I couldn't remember the steps that we took to get there. I didn't care. All I cared about was that we loved each other. And everything else, all of the past pain can go to hell. I will forgive you for all of it. I will forgive my mother. I will forgive my absentee father. Whatever pain I need to let go of I will do it, so long as it doesn't stand in the way of me loving you."

"And Soriya."

"Yes," she said. "And Soriya. But to be honest it's much easier to love a baby than a full-grown man with issues and scars that run deeper than my own. But if I have to do it... If I have to cut myself open again and bleed for you then I will. I love you, Krav. I want you to love me."

"I can't," he said.

"Why not?"

"It's dangerous," he said. "Do you know... Do you know what it's like to desperately want the approval and love of the person who beats you? And to not be able to make that go away? Do you know what that's like? I wish my feelings had died the day they had taken me from my mother's arms. It would've been better. What a sick and twisted thing to pray that you can make the person whose fists leave you battered and bruised love you the way that you love them. He was all that I had. He was all that I had, and I loved him. I wanted to be like him. Until he finally beat it out of me. Only then did I stop loving him. But along with that… It's not easy. To wake up a heart that you have taught to be quiet."

"I am so sorry," she said. "I am so sorry for the way that he hurt you. And it is worse. It's worse than what happened to me. I understand that. It's why I am willing to do this again. Why I am willing to make a fool of myself for you. To consider not my own comfort here. But you have to meet me somewhere."

"No," he said.

She straightened her dress and turned fully to face him, grabbing hold of the sides of his face. "You want this. You wanted it, but you're standing on the edge, afraid to jump in. Afraid to submerse yourself. You're afraid of going all the way with this, and I get that. I do. But we are the only ones that can fix this. No one's going to do it for us. No one else cares enough. You, with all your money and power, you could've remained broken forever if you chose. I am the only one standing here telling you to fix yourself. And you are the only person… Yes, Soriya provided me with clarity. Yes, she made me want to be better. But you were the first thing when I woke up, when I remembered nothing. You were what made me want this life. She has grounded me here. And she gives me purpose. But you matter. Oh, you matter so very much. Please don't forget."

"I…"

"What can I do for you?"

"We should… I should leave you. I should leave you alone for a while. I should…"

"No," she said.

"I can't give you what you want."

"That's okay." A tear slid down her cheek. "That's okay if you can't do it right now. I want it. Please make no mistake. I want it more than I want anything else. For you to love me. No one has ever loved me. No one. Soriya will because she's my child. And you know how that is. I loved my mother. You loved your father. I am grateful for that love. But I have fought hard through the wilderness to be brave enough to love you, Krav. And I want you to love me that same way. I want you to love me enough. But… I'll be patient."

"I don't deserve your patience. I don't need it. *I don't want it.*" He paced back and forth, like a caged animal.

A cage he had built for himself.

"Because you don't know how much you need this. Because you don't understand what love is, do you?"

"I need to go."

"Where?"

"Cambodia. I need to go back there. Because it was the only place that I have her… It's the only place."

"I'll go with you."

"No. I need to go alone."

She shook her head. "We've done this. We've done separation, haven't we? You withdrew from me and I went away. Look what happened. Do you want me out of your life?"

"No."

"It's just that you don't want to love me."

"I don't think I can."

"Let me go with you."

"Damn it," he said. "Damn you to hell, Riot. Can't you just leave me? Can you let me go?"

"Why? So you can try to fix this on your own? So that you can come to all the conclusions about why you don't need to fix it? No. You were able to have me without changing. That was the gift of my amnesia, wasn't it? You could pretend that all the mistakes you made were gone. But I remember them. I know them now. I'm still standing here willing to love you. But you have to do the work. I will stand there with you while you do it. You don't have to be alone in this."

"It's not that simple…"

"It can be. If you'll let it."

"I don't love you."

"Stand in the ruins and tell me that."

And he stood there, rage burning inside of him, anger, at this woman for pushing him. Challenging him. He wanted to tell her to leave him the hell alone.

But he was also terrified of what life might look like if she was gone.

Coward.

She had called him that. Even as she had taken pleasure from him.

And he just wanted… He wanted something else. Something other than what he was. Something other than what they were.

"What about the baby…"

"She was fine without me for a month. She will be okay with the nannies while we do this."

"What if it's for nothing?"

"I'm fighting for you. It will never be nothing. No matter the outcome."

They made arrangements with the staff, and got on the private jet. They barely spoke on the trip over. It was almost like she might have left him. The pain that stretched between them was palpable. The tension. This was like dying.

The only time he had ever felt this way before was after his mother's funeral, but in that case, there was nothing to be done. Nothing to change.

He didn't know what he wanted now. Whether he wanted to be right, or whether he wanted… Her to be right.

It was an endless night. Neither of them slept. They didn't speak. And when they landed in the morning, it wasn't morning there. Just another endless day. And by the time they got out to the temple ruins, the sun was setting again.

He began to walk through the columns, the endless rows of brick and climbing vines.

And he remembered asking her if she was here for a spiritual pilgrimage. As if that was laughable.

"What did you hope to find here?" He looked back at her.

"Myself."

"And you found me instead."

"Yes. But along the way I found myself. I... I thought I was the lamb being led to slaughter. But I'm not. I'm stronger than that. My question is... Are you?"

He didn't know what answers he was looking for, but as they walked through, in total silence, he stopped in front of the remnant of a goddess. And something about it flashed a memory through his mind.

They had something like this. A likeness of the same deity in his home when he was a child. He could scarcely remember. Just like he could scarcely remember his own mother. And suddenly, he could remember feeling. He could remember being in that little house. And everything being right. There was nothing to think about. He was a child, and everything had always been taken care of for him, and he believed that it always would be.

And then...

He remembered... He could remember clinging to his mother's shirt, crying. While they tried to take him away.

And she cried. She screamed, her wailing matching his own.

And they had taken him. They had taken him anyway. He couldn't understand a word they said. He couldn't understand anything. And then there was that man. His father. And he had been... Blisteringly cruel. And he had still longed for his approval. For his affection. For something. Anything.

And all those realizations seemed to pour from him. He wasn't examining them with distance. They were pouring out of him like a flood. Like bleeding.

And he had no control. None at all.

It was just pain. There had been so much pain. And he had chosen to block it out. But he couldn't do that. He couldn't do that and love her. That was the problem. That was the problem.

"I almost lost you," he said. "And you know what that would've done to me?"

"No," she said.

"I wasn't okay. When you were gone. I didn't take another woman to my bed. I didn't want anyone else. I wanted you. Then I found out you were in an accident..."

"And would your detachment have spared you?"

"Maybe. I would... I would never have even known what I felt. I..."

It wasn't raining now. The sun was setting, shining through the ruins, casting her in a glow. And he wondered if he had ever seen colors before. Quite this bright. As the sunrise glinted off her skin. "Because I could never… I could never really see before. I do now."

And it was like blinders had been ripped away. And like every wall had been torn down.

Because of her.

It was work that had started that first moment when he had seen her standing there.

And now it was… Now it was clear. All of it.

"Riot…"

"What?"

It was like seeing for the first time.

"I have lived half a life. Trying to figure out how to keep breathing. But it was only half a life."

"Oh, Krav…"

"I would've not held my child. I would never have had a child. But you. You."

And the lesson was suddenly clear.

He had met her in his weakness. In his vulnerability.

When he was feeling.

"I don't think you can have beauty without pain," he said.

"I'm not sure you can either."

"That night of my mother's funeral… Everything was wrong. I was bombarded with memories that I had spent so many years trying to keep at bay. I was devastated. For all that we could never have. The years taken from us. I felt more in that time than I ever have before. And that was when I met you. And I think it might've been the only moment I ever could have. And I made mistakes. Trying to protect myself still. But I couldn't unlearn what I knew. Which was that feeling was pain. It's taken all this time for me to realize that… I was right. Feeling, loving someone, loving something… It is pain. But that's okay."

"Is it?"

"No. It's not okay. It's terrible. But you make life worth living. These feelings make life worth living."

"Krav."

And it was like that moment, but cast in sunshine. As he walked toward her, as he closed the distance between them, and lowered his head. "I love you."

She could breathe. For the first time in all these hours, she could breathe.

She had decided to hold her ground. She had decided to stand firm, stand with him. They had tried to do things apart. There had been no revelations, only accidents. Stumbling blocks.

And now… Now they were here.

Because they had fought. Because they had emerged from the fray with bloody knuckles and valiant hearts.

He loved her.

"I have all this time. I just couldn't let myself feel it."

"And now?"

"It's like rain. Washing me clean."

"I love you."

"I love you too."

"Let's go to the tree house."

And they did. They made love, and talked about the future. Talked about bringing Soriya here.

"I want to make a life so very different than the one that I lived before."

"It will be easy," she said, tracing her fingers down his chest. "Because we have love."

And he realized, right along with her, that that was the truth of it. That love was the truth of everything. It was what changed hearts, and healed pain. It was what made living worth it.

It was a riot in her soul. And she had made a new meaning for her name. And they had made a new meaning for their lives.

And she knew without a doubt, that here at Angkor Wat, she had found herself.

With him.

Riot Phillips had finally done something spontaneous, and though the road after hadn't been smooth, it had turned out very, very well.

EPILOGUE

THERE WAS NOTHING Krav loved more than watching his children run over the ruins. They were at the tree house, for the summer holidays. It was hot, but everyone was happy. They were tired after a long day spent exploring the mountains, but the children were still running at full speed.

Soriya was lounging on one of the walls, reading a book, for she was eleven and terminally unimpressed with everything.

But she did love stories.

"You know," he said. "I met your mother here."

Soriya lifted her head. "Really?"

"Yes."

"What happened?"

He exchanged a look with Riot across the space. He knew they would have to tell a heavily revised version, that didn't include the fact that they had gone to bed together moments after meeting.

"I saw him," she said. "And I knew he was my fate."

"And how did you know that?"

They exchanged another glance, this one decidedly hot. And he knew they would be spending a long and blissful night in each other's arms. As they had ever since he'd let go of his fear to have her love instead.

"We had the blessing of the rain," he said.

And just like magic, the clouds opened up. And rain began to fall. Hard and cleansing, and perfect. Their four children scattered, and they all ran to the tree house, shivering in the living room and drinking tea, just as he and Riot had done that first night.

"Was that fate?" Soriya asked, wiping raindrops from her forehead, and shaking out her book.

Krav put his arm around Riot and held her close to him. "Yes, yes I do think so. I believe that with us, it always is."

* * * * *

WE HOPE YOU ENJOYED
THIS BOOK FROM
H HARLEQUIN
PRESENTS

Escape to exotic locations where passion knows no bounds.

Welcome to the glamorous lives of royals and billionaires, where passion knows no bounds. Be swept into a world of luxury, wealth and exotic locations.

8 NEW BOOKS AVAILABLE EVERY MONTH!

COMING NEXT MONTH FROM

HARLEQUIN
PRESENTS

#4041 THE KING'S CHRISTMAS HEIR
The Stefanos Legacy
by Lynne Graham
When Lara rescued Gaetano from a blizzard, she never imagined she'd say "I do" to the man with no memory. Or, when the revelation that he's actually a future king rips their passionate marriage apart, that she'd be expecting a precious secret!

#4042 CINDERELLA'S SECRET BABY
Four Weddings and a Baby
by Dani Collins
Innocent Amelia's encounter with Hunter was unforgettable... and had life-changing consequences! After learning Hunter was engaged, she vowed to raise their daughter alone. But now, Amelia's secret is suddenly, scandalously exposed!

#4043 CLAIMED BY HER GREEK BOSS
by Kim Lawrence
Playboy CEO Ezio will do anything to save the deal of a lifetime. Even persuade his prim personal assistant, Matilda, to take a six-month assignment in Greece...as his convenient bride!

#4044 PREGNANT INNOCENT BEHIND THE VEIL
Scandalous Royal Weddings
by Michelle Smart
Her whole life, Princess Alessia has put the royal family first, until the night she let her desire for Gabriel reign supreme. Now she's pregnant! And to avoid a scandal, that duty demands a hasty royal wedding...

HPCNMRA0822

#4045 THEIR DESERT NIGHT OF SCANDAL
Brothers of the Desert
by Maya Blake
Twenty-four hours in the desert with Sheikh Tahir is more than Lauren bargained for when she came to ask for his help. Yet their inescapable intimacy empowers Lauren to lay bare the scandalous truth of their shared past—and her still-burning desire for Tahir...

#4046 AWAKENED BY THE WILD BILLIONAIRE
by Bella Mason
Colliding with a masked stranger at a ball sends shy Emma's pulse skyrocketing. And that's *before* he introduces himself as Alexander Hastings, the CEO with a wild side, which puts him way out of her league! Will Emma step out of the shadows and into the billionaire's penthouse?

#4047 THE MARRIAGE THAT MADE HER QUEEN
Behind the Palace Doors...
by Kali Anthony
To claim her crown, queen-to-be Lise must wed. The man she must turn to is Rafe, the self-made billionaire who once made her believe in love. He'll have to make her believe in it again for passion to be part of their future...

#4048 STRANDED WITH HIS RUNAWAY BRIDE
by Julieanne Howells
Surrendering her power to a man is unacceptable to Princess Violetta. Even *if* that man sets her alight with a single glance! But when Prince Leo tracks his runaway bride down and they are stranded together, he's not the enemy she first thought...

YOU CAN FIND MORE INFORMATION ON UPCOMING HARLEQUIN TITLES, FREE EXCERPTS AND MORE AT HARLEQUIN.COM.

HPCNMRB0822

"Emma," Alex said, pinning her against the wall in a spectacularly graffitied alley, the walls an ever-changing work of art, when he could bear it no more. "I have to tell you. I really don't care about seeing the city. I just want to get you back in my bed."

He could barely believe that he wanted to take her back home. Sending her on her way was the smarter plan. But how smart was it really to deny himself? Emma knew the score. This wasn't about feelings or a relationship. It was just sex.

"Give me the weekend. I promise you won't regret it." His voice was low and rough. He could see in her eyes